BLOW ME A KISS

WILD CANYON ESTATES STORIES, #5

TE SHERIDAN

Blow Me a Kiss

by

TE Sheridan

Contemporary Romance Novella

Published by TE Sheridan

Edited by A. Marie

Cover Photo: Deposit Photos

Cover Design by Redbird Designs

Copyright © 2020 by TE Sheridan

ISBN#: 978-1-951637-13-2

1

———

Bronson Hart flashed a grin—women had swooned at his grin for years, and he knew it—as he twisted the top off a longneck and set the bottle on the makeshift bar. From the corner of his eye, he saw the guy claim the beer and lift it to his mouth, but Bronson kept his focus on the lady. Petite and athletic. Hooded gray eyes and plump, kissable-looking lips.

"Decide?" He arched his eyebrows now as he waited for her to answer. Her soft laughter was thick and warm, and when she tipped her head back, her riotous dark curls flowed around her head. "No hurry."

There wasn't any hurry. Bronson had all night. He could stand here and watch this woman—he hadn't met her before —study the row of craft beer bottles and consider every mixed drink known all night if it took her that long to make a decision. And if he got bored looking at her—he wouldn't; Bronson hadn't met a woman yet who bored him—all he needed to do for entertainment was look around.

Wasn't much to see yet, but within the hour the party would be in full swing, Frank and Donna Jackson's house would be packed, and Bronson would have his pick of women to watch. Not that he needed to see skin to find a woman attractive. But if the women here wanted to strut around in various states of undress, Bronson was going to enjoy the view.

The woman at the bar asked for a glass of pinot. Bronson considered suggesting she start with something a bit stronger. He often made that suggestion to the women, simply because most of them had no idea what sort of party they were attending, and the liquor curbed the anxiety. He poured the pinot without comment, though, since she was here with a date. Maybe being at a Wild Canyon Estates party as part of a couple was a little less daunting than showing up single.

Donna Jackson approached the bar, but she was looking around the open living area. Bronson wished the couple a fun night and turned his attention to Donna. He used to work with her at the bank. And he'd fingered her out back by the pool at one of the first parties. Fucked her a time or two back in the old days, before he'd given up attending the parties as a guest. Their friendship stayed intact; Bronson had no judgment about the activities or the guests who partook in said activities. He'd simply withdrawn from everything after getting the shit stomped and kicked out of his heart. Donna fussed over him at work after the big breakup, and she continued to text him occasionally when he left the bank and went all in with an old college buddy on a startup bar and restaurant. She had said she missed him so often that Bronson thought she was flirting, hinting that she wanted to mess around with him again. Instead, she told him that she and her husband Frank wanted to hire him as their party bartender.

He'd fought it for a week or two, long enough that Donna upped the payment offer so high he couldn't refuse. Not to mention that view. Bronson saw more tits in one night than a frat party did in a weekend. Lot more than that, too. Who needed porn flicks when he could stand behind a bar, sip on good bourbon or a cold beer, and watch real women—short, tall, thin, curvy, black, white—go down on guys, on each other, ride somebody and shake the walls with their orgasms, and then pick up a pay check at the end of the night and go home and wait for next time?

Okay, honestly, there were times he would rather have his own woman. Tucked away in his bed, in his house, all to himself. But it wasn't going to happen, and Bronson had accepted that. Love, kids, blah blah blah—not in the cards for him. He had game, he had that charming smile, and he had—according to several women, Donna included—all the right moves. So, sex wasn't a problem. He could have had his choice of women with the snap of his fingers, but he wasn't that guy. He loved the whole game. The flirting and the conversation and the teasing and the sweet, soft kisses that led to slow, wet kisses that led to roaming hands—

Exactly why he'd had his heart shredded and then swept up in a pile and handed back to him.

Still, he played a little bit at the parties. Not as much as he used to. Mostly, he was okay with watching it all from behind the bar.

"Do you need a drink?" Bronson shuffled down to the end of the bar and leaned over to rest his elbows. "Maybe a shot of Bronson?"

"Is that on the menu?" Donna asked hopefully.

Bronson chuckled.

"Don't tease me." She frowned at him. "It's been a long day."

"So, it sounds like you do need a shot of something stiff."

Donna's laughter rang out loud and happy.

"Just a beer."

No surprise. Neither of the Jacksons drank much on a party night. They ran a tight ship, both of them always observing their guests, making sure everyone had a good time but also ensuring everyone's safety.

Bronson stepped away from her and selected a longneck bottle from the cooler. He twisted the top off, but he didn't relinquish the beer when he stepped closer to her. Donna saw him leaning her way, so she stretched over the bar to meet him halfway. Their lips met in a quick but intimate kiss.

"Maybe you and Frank need to take center stage tonight," he suggested as he had several times before. The hosts did, on occasion, get down and dirty for the rest of them, acting out sexy scenes in the middle of the room. Donna had been married to Frank for as long as Bronson had known her. She loved the guy to the moon and back. But they had opened their marriage to experimentation a few years ago, and then they'd opened their home for others who wanted a safe place to play and experiment with new things and new people. The woman was full-throttle sexy; so much so that Bronson didn't mind looking at Frank's buff shoulders and back and ass or his giant cock when he was doing Donna. Watching the pleasure build in her face, watching her body coil, ready to explode—hearing her scream Frank's name when she came—worth it to Bronson.

"You ready for this?" Donna asked him when she pulled away.

Bronson grinned and took a drink of her beer before handing it over to her.

"You bet I am."

Eyes locked with his, she tipped the bottle up for a drink.

"Do you ever wish things were different?"

Her eyes twinkled. Bronson noticed those little things, too, because he loved everything about women, especially those he considered good friends. A tiny smile played at her lips, but she backed away from the bar as Frank's whistle cut through the pre-party chatter. The constant electronic music was muted while Frank gave the low down on the party for the night. Bronson served another couple as Frank directed the party guests to check their passports. Each had a zoo animal printed on the back, and to find their mate for the night, they had to find a guest with the same animal.

Bronson wondered if there were more than two of each zoo animal represented, but since he was stuck behind the bar all night and didn't carry a party passport, it didn't matter to him. Donna finished the welcome with the usual have-fun, be-open-to-new-things line, and the party goers were off and searching for sex. On cue, the music roared to life again. Bronson straightened as a middle-aged couple approached the bar. He knew them from the parties, knew the guy was a cop and the woman was a teacher. Bronson had laughed when he learned that. Talk about hot for teacher.

He served them their drinks over some small talk. At first, he had thought it was funny that people would engage in idle conversation, especially with him. After all, if the action happened outside by the pool in the warmer months, Bronson saw it. If the action happened in the main living area when the Jacksons moved the bar indoors, Bronson saw it. He hadn't expected people—especially the men—to engage in such explicit behavior and then feel comfortable with talking to him over a drink. Then again, Bronson had done the same a time or two. He had learned quickly that you either lose your inhibitions fast or go home.

"Bronson."

Her voice lit him up inside. With all the sweat-slicked skin and sex he saw at every party, it was this woman who intrigued him to no end. For the last several parties, she had shown up alone, though she visited with a lot of other guests

as if she knew them. Rather than mingle, rather than partici-
pate in the party games, she chose to sit at the bar and chat
with Bronson.

He wouldn't complain. Her big brown eyes drew him in
every damned time. She could have talked about the mating
habits of slugs all night, every night, and he would still be
held captive by those eyes. Her long lashes and the way she
nibbled on her thin lower lip suggested vulnerability, even
though her long, slender fingers and her lithe body appeared
strong, even tough. She always seemed comfortable in her
skin, in her clothing—always a mix of classy and trendy and
a little bit sexy—and she liked to talk. Bronson hung on her
every word, never mind that her voice was soft and sweet.
She made him laugh with her interesting observations and
snide comments—not about other party guests, but current
events or news items.

"Violet." He stilled at the bar directly across from her. "I
was hoping you would be here."

"How could I miss a date with my favorite bartender?"
Her lips tipped up in a small, shy smile. Now and then, she
tiptoed up to flirting, but she had never jumped into
anything headfirst. With him or anyone else here, as far as he
knew. Her fingers were bare; she wore a silver bracelet on
her left wrist and no other jewelry.

"Do you know a lot of bartenders?" He tipped his head
and studied her curiously. Tonight, she wore a silver tank
with an oversized deep, lush green cardigan. He hadn't seen
her approach, but he knew without looking that she wore
dark wash denim that hugged her shapely legs and ass, most
likely black ankle boots, and Bronson had no idea, but he
liked to imagine her in sexy lingerie, starting with a black
lace thong.

"A couple," she said with a grin.

"But I'm your favorite?" He arched his brows hopefully,

his blood already roaring through his body with the force of a volcano exploding.

"Yep." She laughed softly as she shifted to settle on one of only three stools at the bar.

"Well, you're my favorite patron," he told her. He knocked on the bar, glad it was there to stand behind. Maybe this was a party where no one would think twice if he popped a tent in his jeans, but something told him Violet was different. She might be offended if she knew the thoughts that tore through his mind like a roller coaster that had jumped its tracks whenever she was around. "Definitely my favorite sight at a Wild Canyon party."

"Right." This time her laugh was a bit louder, freer. "I don't need any lines, Bronson. Just a drink."

He considered arguing, promising her that it wasn't a line. After being a guest at the first several parties and then tending bar the past couple of years here, he had seen it all. Done it all. He wouldn't complain about the scenery, but he was much more interested in the brunette sitting at the bar now than all the skin around her.

"The usual?" he asked her.

Violet—he didn't know her last name—usually drank a glass of chardonnay. Now and then, she sipped two as she sat and talked to him. What he wouldn't give to serve her a third. Not to get her drunk, but to keep her there with him just a bit longer.

She studied him now, almost flirtatiously, with her eyes narrowed and the hint of a smile on her pale, thin lips. His dick surged to life again, but he reminded himself he was just the bartender. He had no idea why this woman had started attending Frank and Donna's parties; in all of their conversation, they had never gotten too personal. But she obviously wasn't interested in free sex, and just because she sat at the bar and regaled him with her tales of travels and her commentary on life, that certainly didn't mean she was into him.

"Surprise me," she said with a small shake of her head.

"Really?" He tipped his head and eyed her skeptically.

"Really." She nodded. Bronson lowered his gaze in time to see her perfect white teeth scrape over her lower lip.

"You got it." He nodded as he rubbed his hands together and turned to eye the liquor bottles.

"You can't get me drunk," she called to him, still laughing, and Bronson thought wistfully, still flirting.

"They won't let you drive home if you fail the Breath-a-lyzer." He waved her words and her concern away as he selected a bottle of rye whiskey.

"Well, then how would I get home?"

"I'll take you." He looked at her over his shoulder and flashed her a grin.

Their eyes met, and Bronson noticed the tiniest flair of her nostrils, the widening of her eyes. Was she flirting? Could this woman be interested in him? She broke the eye contact to look at the bottle in his hands.

"Rye?" She winced.

"Do you like margaritas?"

"Yeah, but—"

"Just a little twist," he said softly. "Trust me."

She snapped her eyes back up to meet his, all trace of teasing gone.

"I do." She nodded.

His blood a raging fire through his veins now, Bronson nodded slowly. He wondered what she would do if he took her by the hand and led her down the hall to the mudroom. If he pressed her up against the wall there in the midst of the Jacksons' closets and washer and dryer and worked her lips over with his own? With his teeth? What if he unzipped her jeans and slipped his hands inside them? Would she be into him?

He didn't want it that way.

Not with her.

He'd had his share of wall sex at these parties and in other places. He'd had his share of blowjobs behind this bar. He'd had his share of kissing outside in the pool. And he would very much like to do all of the above with Violet. But not yet.

Bronson wanted to romance her.

He wanted the thrill of the chase, the buildup to something more.

He turned away from her as the thought hit him. He wanted something more. Sure, he had always assumed that one day he would be the guy with a wife and a kid or two. Figured he'd coach little league soccer or baseball and have snowball fights with his kids and fix Sunday brunch for his wife. But after Jillian Keane had broken his heart, he'd shelved all of those thoughts, walked away from the parties, and lived like a monk for a while.

Naturally, he eventually found he needed sex, but he hadn't wanted *more* since then.

Violet made him want more.

Unsettled—fuck that—*baffled* by his attraction to her and more by his need for her, he turned away from her to fix her drink that was similar to a margarita. He figured she would like it, and if she didn't, he would simply fix her something else.

"Try this."

She stirred from her thoughts—she'd been turned sideways, eyes directed at the closed French doors—and looked back at him

"You okay?" she asked him, a curious frown on her face.

"I'm good." He grinned, determined to shake off the weird, heavy thoughts that had stolen in a second ago.

"What is it?"

"Just taste it."

He leaned over, rested his elbows on the bar as she picked up the glass. Bronson watched with a growing hunger, fixated on her fingers around the glass and then her lips as she sipped. He wondered what the drink would taste like on her lips and then decided he was going to have to deal with a hard-on for the rest of the night.

Slowly, she lowered the glass to the bar. Bronson watched her savor the drink for a moment, watched her swallow it, and then lifted his gaze to meet her eyes.

"What do you think?" he asked her. Her fingers were still curled around the glass. Desperate to touch her, to see if her skin was as warm and soft as he thought it would be, he moved his hand just enough to brush his fingertip over her knuckles.

Was it his imagination, or did she gasp softly at his touch?

"Not sure yet." She rubbed her lips together, drawing his attention away from her eyes. If she licked her lips right now, he decided, it meant something. The party was blowing up around them; in his peripheral vision, Bronson saw three couples already in various stages of making out. Music pounded around them, and at any moment, someone would approach the bar for a drink and break the spell he and Violet were under.

But this moment was just for them.

"Tequila," he told her. "Little bit of whiskey."

"Do you like it?" she asked him. His fingertip rested on the back of her right ring finger. Eyes locked again, Bronson nodded. He liked the drink. He liked the woman. He liked the contact. Whatever she was asking, yes was the only answer.

She lifted the glass again and sipped. Bronson watched her, intrigued by the pensive look on her face as she savored the liquor and swallowed. This time when she put the glass down, she let go of it. A wave of warmth engulfed him when she stretched her fingers out to touch his.

"It's good," she decided.

"I didn't make it too strong," he promised her.

"Because you don't want to drive me home?" She tipped her head and offered him a coy smile. The warmth fired up to inferno when she parted her lips and wet them with the tip of her tongue.

"Because I want you to sit here all night," he answered. "And talk to me."

She considered his words as all the blood in his body continued to pound painfully hard in his cock. Bronson would drive her home in a heartbeat. He'd walk her to her door and kiss her goodnight. But he wanted more than a hookup that lasted a night or two. So, rather than get her drunk enough to drive her home, he wanted her to be here with him all night.

"Okay." She nodded.

Both of them tipped their chins at the same time to study their fingers just inches apart now on the bar top. Bronson lifted his just as she did. Electric awareness hummed on his skin as they linked fingers.

Funny. It would be perfectly acceptable at this party for her to join him behind the bar. For him to go to his knees in front of her. But Bronson was thrilled at the simple act of holding hands with her.

As if she felt the same way, she gave him a gentle squeeze. He lifted his gaze from their hands to meet her eyes again. The smile on her face made him feel ten feet tall. He wanted more than cheap sex, and that little gesture—the squeeze— made him think maybe Violet did too.

"Bronson."

The voice was a bucket of ice water over the warmth Violet had stirred in him.

"Baby, I am so glad to see you."

Violet tried to pull her hand away from him, but he held on for a second, returned the gentle pressure on her fingers before letting her go and looking to the right at the redhead watching him with big, hungry green eyes.

"Jillian."

2

She looked good, but then so did all the women here. But none of them, Jillian Keane included, compared to Violet. Bronson felt a pang—not a pain, but a knife of regret —in his chest when Violet slowly drew her hand away from his. Most likely, Jillian didn't notice. She couldn't notice, because like most of the women here tonight, Jillian was probably on the prowl for some sexy fun. The Wild Canyon Estates parties were all about cutting loose and letting off steam after a stressed work week or month. No one came here looking for anything lasting, definitely not love.

But at the moment, Bronson was looking for something more than a casual hookup, and Jillian's magic act of appearing in his life right now—ta da!—was less than welcome.

"Hi, Jill." He straightened and turned to his ex, though he didn't move away from Violet. Aware of the quiet brunette watching him as he spoke to Jillian, he reminded himself to proceed with caution. He and Jillian had been over for a long time, but Violet didn't know that. She didn't know anything about his past, and he didn't want her to think less of him for mistreating a woman.

Ah, hell, he didn't *want* to mistreat Jillian. She'd walked away from him, yes, leaving him broken. He didn't love her anymore, and her timing was awful, but he wouldn't treat her rudely, either. It wasn't his game. How to convey all of that to Violet without cramming it all into a conversation right this instant?

He couldn't. He wouldn't even try.

Instead, he reached for her hand and brushed his fingers over hers. A signal to Jillian, maybe. But more than that, he wanted Violet to know he was interested in her. That he liked where they were headed a minute ago before they were interrupted.

"You haven't changed," Jillian marveled as she unabashedly gave him the once over. Bronson tipped his head at her just enough to convey his impatience. "You look as delicious as ever."

He fought the desire to glance at Violet. Jillian meant nothing by the comment; she wasn't trying to get under Violet's skin or throw a wrench in the conversation they had been having a moment ago. It wouldn't occur to her that something might be happening there, something other than flirting and possibly a blowjob or three-minute encounter in the pantry.

"How've you been?" he asked as he snagged a bottle of top shelf vodka. "It's been a while, Jillian."

He splashed the clear liquid into a small glass tumbler and then pushed it over the counter at his ex. Dressed in a black pantsuit cut low enough to broadcast that she wasn't wearing a bra, it was obvious to Bronson that she wouldn't be sticking around the bar long. She was looking for a good time, and once she understood that she wasn't going to find it with Bronson, she would move on.

"Good." She picked up the glass and sipped from it. "But I've missed you."

Bronson had no comment. He was relieved when a familiar-looking guy approached the bar and asked for a beer. He shared a second or two of small talk with him as he twisted the top off the bottle, but his ear was trained to the women at his left. Jillian had introduced herself to Violet. No doubt she was looking for Violet's passport to see if their zoo animals were a match. Jillian hadn't been choosy back when they were together; Bronson assumed she was still into women and men both.

Bronson heard Violet give Jillian her name—just her first name. He inched back down the bar to them, pleased to see that Violet was sipping on the drink he had made for her.

"Are you new here?" Jillian asked Violet. Bronson bristled when he saw Jillian's eyes dip and slide south over Violet's body. Was she sizing her up to put the moves on her? Would Violet be into that?

"You haven't been to a party in a long time, Jill," Bronson reminded her in an attempt to protect Violet if she didn't want to answer.

"We moved to Rockfield a few months ago," Violet answered simply. "Frank invited me the first time in August."

News to Bronson. He always found it interesting to hear whether a guest was here at Frank's or Donna's invitation. Wondered if that meant the hosts were interested in the guests or simply thought the people they invited would enjoy the party activities.

He wondered now who the *we* was that Violet had referred to. Was she married? Had he missed seeing her walk in with someone each night? Or was there someone waiting at home for her on nights like this?

He swept his gaze over her hands again, relieved for a second to see no rings. But a flash of skin behind Jillian and

Violet reminded him rings didn't particularly matter in this world. Vows. Rings. Titles. Everyone here was willing to look the other way for a few hours to fulfill sexual fantasies. Maybe Violet was no different.

"Donna didn't tell you I was coming, did she?" Jillian turned back to him. Glass at her lips, she kept her eyes on him as he remembered Donna's earlier question. *Did he ever wish things were different?*

He did, yes.

But that didn't mean he wished he was with Jillian Keane. "No."

Jillian nodded. She set her drink down and reached for his hand. Resigned to the moment, Bronson leaned over the bar so she could kiss him. Her lips were warm and soft on the corner of his mouth, but the kiss did nothing for him. Back in the day, he had been all over this woman on a daily basis. He'd been infatuated with her body, thought he would love her forever, and she had made a fool of him.

"Catch up with you later," she whispered. Bronson sighed and held his tongue as she snagged her drink and sauntered away from the bar. He needed a moment before returning to Violet. Not because of any action in his pants, but because he didn't want to turn to Violet and dump the sordid affair at her feet. Happy to mix a couple of martinis at the opposite end of the bar, he chatted with a couple about how fast time was flying and how could it possibly be November already.

When he did make his way back down the bar, Violet was studying her drink. She didn't look angry, or jealous, even. Bronson felt a stab of relief and maybe a touch of disappointment at that. He didn't want drama; at this stage in the game, he had no interest in drama or a one-sided relationship with one person clinging to the other who wasn't particularly interested. But as he watched her, he admitted to himself that he had hoped for a bit of interest, at least, in who Jillian was to him.

"Do they do these parties all year?" She lifted her gaze from the drink and studied him silently. "Because I'm just wondering how the Christmas party looks. If Santa makes an appearance."

The slight curve of her lips took his breath away for a second. He might have hoped for a flicker of jealousy, maybe, but this could be better. Judging from the slight arch in her eyebrow and the hint of a smile, she was sliding back to the easy, flirty conversation they were having before Jillian interrupted them.

"You missed the Halloween party." He wagged his brows at her and drew a soft laugh. Eyes on her lips again, Bronson forced himself to take a deep breath.

"Yeah." She lifted one shoulder in a lazy shrug. "Had other commitments. Was it crazy?"

"I'd say yes, but…" He made a show of looking around the living area before meeting her gaze again. "It's all pretty crazy here, right?" He wanted to ask what commitments had kept her from coming here to hang out with him, but he didn't.

Violet tipped her head to acknowledge what he said, but she didn't necessarily agree, either.

"People are interesting," she finally mumbled. "Were there costumes?"

"For the first five minutes of the party." He nodded, lifted a finger to indicate that he would be right back, and moved away to serve the two girls who approached.

"And you?" Violet asked when he returned to her end of the bar.

"Me? What? Am I interesting?"

"Oh, you're interesting, Bronson." She pursed her lips and then laughed at the surprise on his face. "Did you—"

"Wait." He leaned into the bar and shook his head. "What? What does that mean?"

"What does what mean?"

"I'm interesting. What do you mean?"

Violet studied him again, this time with narrowed eyes, as if she were looking for something or hoping to memorize his face. Eventually, she looked away, a mix of amused and embarrassed, and lifted her drink.

"What's a guy like you doing behind that bar every night? Wouldn't you rather be out here on this side? Partaking in the…" She threw a long look over her shoulder before swinging her gaze back to him. "Activities."

"Nothing wrong with the view from back here."

She barked a loud laugh and nodded. "I'm sure there isn't." She hunched her shoulders and leaned into the bar. "But is it enough?"

"Are you worried about me, Violet?"

"Are you married?" she asked him.

Bronson blinked at her, surprised and a little bit thrilled by her question. Finally, they were going to move into a more personal discussion.

"I'm not," he answered.

"Would you be here if you were?"

He eyed the wistful look on her face and then glanced at her drink. Was it the liquor talking? She'd never seemed curious about any of this before.

"No." He shrugged. "Unless my wife was here, too."

"Would you want your wife to be here?"

Her whisper was a like an intimate caress. Bronson had to concentrate to hold down the shiver.

"No."

Maybe the question wouldn't have bothered him if Jillian hadn't picked tonight to show up out of nowhere. As it was, it poked a little too close for comfort. He stepped back from

Violet and eyed his supplies behind the bar. Everything from the liquor to the cocktail napkins to the stir sticks was completely in order. There was nothing pressing to take him away from Violet, but he needed some space.

He felt her eyes on him as he dug a longneck from the cooler. Ice chips slid off the bottle as he twisted the top off. Too bad he wasn't hot and bothered right now. If anything, he was frustrated. Reminded again of the way Jillian had wrecked what he had thought was their perfect future.

"So, bride or groom?" Violet asked suddenly.

"What?" Bronson did a double take. He took a swig from the beer and then chased it with a deep breath. Violet had no idea the things that had happened in his past; she hadn't poked the bear to hurt him. She was either interested in him or trying to make sense of why she continued to show up at the Wild Canyon Estates parties.

"Who hired you? Donna or Frank?"

He felt his lips curve in a lazy grin. Easy question, but if Violet continued on this road, she would eventually ask if Bronson had been intimate with Donna. He wasn't ashamed of what he and Donna had done, but, he wasn't sure he was ready to share that with Violet. Again, this hardly seemed the place for that sort of conversation. Not if he hoped this was the start of something.

And he did.

"Donna."

"You knew her...before?"

Bronson chuckled, pulled in one more deep cleansing breath, and settled across from Violet again.

"I worked with her."

"So, were you a party guest first?"

He nodded without comment.

Violet stared at him boldly. He had no idea what she was thinking, but he was dying to know.

"Wild Canyon's not the only crazy circus out there." She arched her eyebrows, but she lowered her gaze to her drink. Bronson waited for her to say more, but her silence niggled at him. The music blared around them; Bronson noticed a change in the song, but the rest was the same. Donna stood by the French door with Susan Hooper at the moment—both of them fully clothed, but everywhere else he looked, he saw skin.

"Did you dress up? For Halloween?" Chin still tucked, she looked at him through long, thick lashes.

"As a bartender," he answered with a straight face. "What kept you from being here?"

She shook her head, apparently unwilling to share personal information, even though she was lobbing questions at him left and right.

"What about you?" He tried again.

Violet lifted her chin this time and picked up her glass. Bronson watched her drink again. She met his gaze; the flick of her tongue over her lips rendered him breathless. Cue the hot and bothered part.

"What about me?"

"You said Frank invited you here," he reminded her.

"I didn't tell you that."

"I heard you tell Jillian."

"I don't work with him if that's what you're asking."

Bronson waited her out. What did that mean? If she didn't work with him, how did she know Frank?

"I met with him when we first moved here," she said quietly. "He closed on the house."

"So, you're his client?"

"I was." She nodded.

"And he just up and invited you here?"

There was more to it. Obviously, there was more. But it

was just as obvious she had no intention of explaining it to him when she simply nodded.

Frustrated all over again, although this time it had nothing to do with Jillian, Bronson lifted his hand to squeeze the back of his neck.

"Do you need another one?" He nodded to her empty glass.

"No. Thanks." She nudged it his way and then looked around. He recognized the move. She was going to leave. What the hell had he said to run her off?

"Wine?"

"No." She turned back to him with a tired smile. "I'm actually going to head out."

"Why?"

"What?" His bold question seemed to take her by surprise. Bronson might have started this night content to flirt with her and watch her walk away again, but he decided now that he wasn't ready for the night to end. The teasing, the flirting, tonight felt a bit like she'd kissed him and run.

"Why are you leaving so soon? You just got here."

"What time do you get done here?"

"It's different every time," he said quietly.

"Do you leave alone?" She glanced backward over her shoulder but looked back at him almost instantly. Was she looking for Jillian? Was she jealous? Is that why she was leaving so soon?

"I do."

She quirked an eyebrow at him suggestively, but Bronson had no idea what it meant. If she had asked him to meet her in the mudroom, he would walk away from the bar to do it. To suggest a different time and meeting place. But he couldn't just walk out of the party and leave Frank and Donna in the lurch.

"Don't go." He touched the back of her hand, relieved when she didn't pull away from him.

Violet reached for the little black clutch purse she carried. Bronson watched her unzip it and slip a small notepad and pen from it. She jotted something down and then pushed the paper over the bar toward him.

Bronson took the paper, but he kept his eyes on her as she put the items back, zipped her purse again, and slipped off the barstool.

"Goodnight, Bronson."

3

The front window of the small bungalow was lit with a golden glow despite the hour. Bronson hesitated at the drive, uncertain if he should pull in or park at the curb. When he called the number she'd written down for him, she had simply asked if he wanted to come by. Parking at the curb seemed to be a better choice, so Bronson pulled to the curb and climbed out of his SUV. Thankfully, the party had wrapped up just after midnight; there were nights when they dragged well into the small hours. He'd had the bar closed and cleaned up before the last guest left, and he was out the door after quick goodbyes with Donna and Frank.

The welcome mat in front of the door was a nondescript beige. The front door itself was a thick, old oak. Bronson lifted a hand to buzz the doorbell, but he hesitated when he remembered that Violet had used the pronoun *we* more than once earlier tonight. Before that thought could sink in, the knob twisted and the lock popped, and Violet pulled the door open.

She was still dressed as she had been for the party, though she'd kicked off the boots and now had her jeans tucked into thick, cozy socks. Her eyes glowed in a tired face, and behind her, warm lamplight beckoned him inside.

"Hi." Her smile was a bit shy, but she stepped back to let him in. Though he was a bit chilled from being outside, he moved hesitantly. This was something different. Flirting with Violet at the parties was easy; her invitation spoke volumes about trust. But he wasn't certain what she was thinking when she'd invited him over, and that uncertainty nagged at him.

"Hi."

"Is this early?" She stepped around him to close the door and then moved in front of him to lead him further into the room. "I thought the parties probably went on all night long."

"Some do." He nodded.

"Can I get you something to drink?" she offered.

Bronson spotted a nearly empty wineglass on an end table by the sofa. There was also a crème-colored throw tossed aside and a paperback book propped open near the glass. Was she always a night owl, or had she stayed up waiting to hear from him?

"Some people wouldn't forgive you for that." He ran his finger down the cracked spine of the book and then glanced at her. The rueful smile on her face lit him up inside.

"It's a used book," she promised him. "The spine looked like that when I picked it up."

"Garage sale?"

"Used bookstore." She shook her head. "Garage sales depress me."

"Why's that?"

She shrugged and folded her arms over her chest. "I don't know. I think it's sad to let things go. And so often, the sale's a result of a loss or a breakup."

Bronson eyed her curiously.

"Maybe it's just downsizing," he offered. "Moving to a new city. Upward and onward."

Violet grinned. "Maybe."

"You read thrillers?" he asked her.

"What did you think I would read?" She tipped her head. "Romance?"

"I honestly can't read you, so I have no idea what I would have said," he said truthfully. "And for the record, I like romances now and then."

"Books or real life?"

"Both."

She laughed softly. "You're ruining my plans for the night."

"How so?"

"I offered you a drink," she reminded him.

"So you could get me drunk? Have your way with me?"

Her laughter was sweet music.

"No. I just thought I would get you wine or bourbon, and we could just sit. And talk."

"Talk."

She dragged her teeth over her lower lip.

"The parties are fun, but it's hard to have a real conversation."

"True," he agreed.

"Do you have someone to go home to?" She arched her brows. "Or can you can stay for a while?"

"I'm not married," he said. "I told you that."

"But you could have someone at home waiting."

"No." He shook his head and shrugged out of his leather bomber jacket.

"Wine? Or bourbon?"

"Whatever you're having," he told her.

Bronson watched her graceful movements as she took a glass from a cabinet above her head and picked up a half empty bottle of red. Before she could put the stopper back in the bottle, he snatched her glass from the end table and brought it to her for a refill.

"Thank you." She smiled at him as they swapped glasses.

"I have to ask."

He watched her sip and then lick her lips. She shrugged and nodded, as if to say ask away.

"Earlier, you told Jillian that you'd moved here a while ago. But you used the word *we*."

"I'm not married," she answered immediately.

Bronson shrugged and cocked his head as if to remind her of what she had just said to him.

"I'm divorced, Bronson," she said softly. "My little girl and I moved here to be closer to my mother."

Bronson drank from his glass and considered her words.

"Does that make you regret being here?"

"Not at all." He shook his head. "She's not here now. Is she?"

"She goes to my mom's when I have plans. Actually, she sleeps over at my mom's once a weekend, whether I have plans or not." Violet shrugged her eyebrows sadly. "She's got a bigger social life than I do."

"How old is she?"

"Seven."

"Second grade."

"Do you have kids?"

"No." He paced the room, eyes moving from Violet's face to the framed pictures scattered through the room and back to Violet. "Never married. No kids. Just nieces and nephews."

"Avery's a great kid." She swallowed hard. "I was really worried about her, about how she would handle the move, but she's done well."

"And your ex?" Bronson asked.

"What about him?"

"Does she see him?"

Violet winced. She made her way around the sofa to sit down and stared up at him until he joined her. Bronson sat close, but he was careful not to crowd her. She sipped her wine again, put her glass on the end table, and then twisted to sit sideways and look at him.

"Yes and no." She rested her head on the cushion for a minute and then lifted her head and took a deep breath. "Yeah, she sees him. Kody tries with her. He's not a bad guy. But..."

"But?"

Violet cleared her throat. Bronson noticed her shoulders hitch in a slight shrug, wondered why she wouldn't look him in the eyes now. She picked up the book and folded the corner of her page down before she closed it.

"Do you read?" She smoothed her hand over the cover and finally looked up at him. Her big brown eyes hit him in the heart. Bronson decided to forgive the change in subject. For now.

"I read political thrillers. Mysteries."

"Hmm." She studied his face. "I would have pegged you for sci-fi."

"Why sci-fi?" He lowered his gaze to watch her teeth graze her lip again.

"I don't know." She spoke quietly, but her eyes watched him boldly. "I should have known. You're kind of mysterious."

"Me?" He laughed and tossed his hand up defensively, careful not to spill his wine. "I'm an open book."

"Yeah?" She pressed her lips together and quirked her eyebrow. "You're a sexy bartender. Is that it?"

"You think I'm sexy?"

"I do," she confessed. She held his gaze a moment longer

and then dipped her head enough to break the eye contact. "I'm just curious what's underneath that façade."

"Unfortunately, it's not a façade," he said quietly. "I tend bar at the very adult Wild Canyon Estates parties, and by day, I run a bar and grill."

She tilted her head just enough that he could see the smirk on her face.

"Do you cook?"

"I can, but not at the bar and grill, no."

"Hmm."

"What else do you want to know?"

"Dream car."

"Mmm." He frowned as he considered her question. "Chevelle…Nineteen seventy. Black with white stripes.

"That's pretty specific."

"It's a muscle car—"

"I know what it is." She cut him off with a nod.

"Had one when I was nineteen. I'd love to have it back."

"What happened to it?"

"Wrecked it."

"Mmm."

"Boys will be boys." He shrugged and offered her an embarrassed grin. "Me and a couple of buddies were drag racing. I lost control. Totaled it."

"Were you injured?"

"Yes, ma'am, I was. Broken wrist and a broken leg. I don't recommend it."

She chuckled. "Broke my wrist when I was twelve."

"Drag racing?" He narrowed his eyes at her and felt something warm and intoxicating unfurl in him when she rewarded him with a laugh.

"No. Roller skating."

"Speed skating, though, right?"

She laughed softly and shook her head. "Well, the kid that

ran into me and sent me sprawling might have been speed skating."

Bronson watched her take a drink and then study the ruby liquid in her glass.

"What else?" He nudged her knee with the back of his hand.

"Hobbies."

"Ummm." He shrugged and shook his head. "I work out? Does that count? I read."

"That's it?"

"I might get crazy on a Saturday night and watch a movie. Binge watch TV now and then."

She studied him suspiciously for a moment. "Do you play games?"

Bronson hesitated. Was she still talking about hobbies? As in board games? Card games? Maybe because she was thinking about her daughter? Or was she asking him if he played games with women?

"I used to play Chess with my grandpa," he told her, but he screwed his face up into a frown. "I wasn't very good at it, and I didn't like it. I do like to play rummy, though."

"Poker?"

"Nah." He shook his head. "Haven't played in a good twenty years. And that was with high school buddies. We were just screwing around." He laughed, but he sobered up when he caught the cool look in her eyes. "Same buddies I was with when I wrecked my car."

"Mm." She nodded. "Drugs?"

"No." He stretched and leaned past her to set his glass on the table by hers. She ducked her head when he was close enough to feel her breath on his face. Bronson breathed deeply, lost in her scent. He had no idea what it was, but the closest he could come was coconut. He liked coconut, but Violet smelled a hell of a lot better than coconut lotion.

"I've…" She whooshed out a sigh and lifted her chin as he sank back to his spot on the couch. "Been so careful." She shrugged. "Since…"

"Since what?" He ached to touch her, to take her in his arms and pull her into his lap. She had folded in on herself, though, as they talked. Knees under her and shoulders hunched, almost like she was afraid of him. He counted to ten, reminded himself he had all the time in the world if she needed to move slowly.

"The divorce?" She sounded uncertain. "Not because… Not for me. But." She shrugged and licked her lips. "For Avery."

"Okay."

"It's been fourteen months."

Bronson stared at her silently for a moment, trying to read between the lines. Fourteen months since the divorce was final? Since she'd been with anyone? Was she interested in him? But still skittish to start something? Obviously, she trusted him. That trust swelled inside him and made his heart hammer in his ribs, but it worried him, too. What if she had found herself attracted to someone else? At the party? Or anywhere? What if she had invited the wrong person in?

"Since?"

But Violet only nodded.

Bronson waited for her to say something, to make the next move. He felt a little hitch in his breath when she straightened suddenly and reached for his hand. Willing his dick to stand down, willing his body into patience, he linked his fingers with hers and waited. The flash of courage gone, Violet kept her eyes on their joined hands, her thumb rubbing back and forth over his knuckles.

"I'm sorry." She laughed softly. Bronson assumed that whatever she had in mind when she asked him to come by now seemed like a bad idea to her. That she'd changed her mind and maybe now she was afraid he would be angry with her.

"Don't apologize."

"I don't know if I was ever very good at his," she whispered, "but I feel like I'm doing it all wrong now."

"I'm not even sure what you're doing, but I promise you there doesn't have to be a right or wrong way."

She tipped her head to look at him through her lashes.

"If you're not sure what I'm doing, then obviously, I'm not doing it right."

"What if I told you something?" He dragged in a deep breath and ducked his head.

"What?"

"I've been attracted to you since the first time you walked into Donna and Frank's house."

When Violet gently tugged her hand away from his, he wished he could take the words back. He had a hundred questions for her, but he didn't want to know her dream car or what her hobbies were. He was more interested in why her marriage had ended and what the fourteen months she had referred to was about.

She didn't get up, though. She didn't ask him to leave. For a moment, she simply held his gaze with hers. Finally, she surprised him and moved slowly but gracefully to straddle his lap. Reminding himself again to be patient, to let her lead, Bronson couldn't stop his hands from settling on her hips.

Violet lifted her hand to stroke her fingers over his lips. Bronson watched her eyes follow the movement and then fixate on his mouth. She pressed the pad of her thumb to the center of her lower lip, her fingers skimming the scruff on his cheek.

Breathless, but more than pleased with her interest in his lips, he parted them slightly and rested his head on the sofa cushion. Violet lifted her eyes to meet his; the fire, the heat, in her gaze burned through him, but he didn't want to scare her away.

He flicked her thumb with the tip of his tongue, stunned when she drew it away and licked it herself.

"I can think of better ways to do that." His words came out more like a growl, but the heat in her eyes only flickered hotter. Eyes on his, she leaned into him, only closing hers when she was close enough that he could feel her breath on his lips. Bronson was aware of her mouth almost on his, his heartrate jumping through the roof, and his cock throbbing with the need to touch her. To lift his hips and grind into her.

It hurt when she kissed him. His heart pounded so fucking hard, it hurt. Just the press of her closed lips on his was going to kill him. Her hair fell over her face and brushed his nose, his cheek, as she continued with the curious, suggestive kisses.

"Is this okay?" Her fingers were magically on the back of his neck now, moving up and down with the same sort of touch as her lips on his. Barely there, a delicious whisper of something that felt incredible. She shifted slightly in his lap, and suddenly, his cock was tucked in the vee of her thighs. The heat there between their bodies threatened to burn, making him incapable of coherent thought.

Instead of answering her, Bronson simply parted his lips and stroked hers with his tongue. The tiny mewl in the back of her throat gripped his dick and his heart. She kissed him back, open mouthed, with her tongue sliding over his, like he was water and she was dying of thirst.

Bronson heard himself groan with content when those fingers on the back of his neck squeezed gently. She kissed him again and again, each pass, each kiss longer, searching for more. He wanted to stand, to carry her in his arms to her bedroom, and strip her naked. If she liked kissing like this, he would be happy to lay her out and kiss her everywhere.

"Are you sure?" His voice was gruff when he broke the kiss. She moaned in protest and turned her head, offering him her neck. Bronson nipped at her earlobe and rubbed his nose over her neck, down to her collarbone.

"Please."

His hands moved again before his brain could decide if it was a good idea. He stroked his fingers up under the tail of her tank and bit off a curse at the feel of her soft, warm skin. Violet's eyes fluttered closed as he dragged his knuckles around to her front, tracing the waistline of her jeans.

"You're beautiful." He pressed his open mouth to her neck again and nipped at her.

"Bronson." She gasped at the touch of his fingertip on her nipple. Bronson cupped her breast, the curve heavy in his hand under the soft lace. With a desperate moan, she drew her hands away from him. He stilled, one hand on her breast and the other curled around her side, but she only shrugged out of the sweater and let it fall to the floor.

"We don't have to rush this." His whisper was gruff with need. He didn't want to rush through something he'd been fantasizing about for months. But with her heat straddling his cock and her breast in his hand, the thought of stopping was a physical pain.

Her eyes were glazed now with lust, her lips swollen from his kisses. His promise that they didn't have to rush unheard or ignored, Violet dropped her hands to her waist. Bronson watched her gather the tank in her hands and slide it up in one smooth, tantalizingly slow motion and take it off. The sight of her full breasts and the black lace under his hand, spiked his heartrate again. His cock like a steel rod, he lifted his eyes to hers.

4

———

Bronson watched as she reached to slide her bra straps from her shoulders, her hooded eyes still locked with his. The black straps loose on her upper arms and the curves of her breasts spilling over the top of the lace cups, he molded his hands over her sides and around her back to deal with the hook. Violet's lips parted in a silent moan when he plucked the lace from her chest and let it fall to the floor. Eyes still locked with his, she took his hands in hers.

Expecting her to put them on her breasts, Bronson was surprised when she lifted first his left hand to her mouth to kiss his palm. The soft, warm kiss on his skin filled him with longing. He watched with growing need when she turned her mouth to his other hand and kissed it, too.

He grunted like an animal when she flicked her tongue in the center of his hand and then traced his fingers, one by one, slowly, as if savoring each one. Her sultry stare was both bold and defiant, as if she expected him to pull away from her. Unable to hold back any longer, he lowered his gaze to her bare breasts. The feel of her eyes on him as he drank in the sight sent another jolt of lust straight to his cock.

Her breasts were perfectly round, and her nipples tightened as he admired her. His right hand still in hers, her lips now whispering kisses over his knuckles, Bronson gently palmed her breast in his other. A hiss of approval, maybe, or a demand for more, escaped her parted lips. Bronson felt her warm breath over his wet knuckles.

"Violet." He reshaped her breast and finally captured her nipple between his finger and thumb. She cried out and arched into his hand. Bronson felt her teeth scrape over his knuckles as she moved to her knees to lean into him.

"More." Her whispered demand threw him into motion. Violet still held his hand at her lips and when he dipped his head to brush his mouth over the curve of her breast, she bit him, her teeth sinking in hard, her moan like a salve on the sting.

The wet warmth of her mouth on his hand was erotic. His cock throbbed, desperate for the same. But his need to hold her in his hands, to cup her breasts and lift them to his own mouth, spurred him into action. He drove his fingers—still wet from her kisses—around her neck and up into her hair and tugged her close to slant his mouth over hers. Violet rewarded him by wrapping her arms around his shoulders, her fingers playing in his close-cropped hair, her breasts pressed to his chest. She surrendered to his kiss and met his tongue thrust for thrust.

When Bronson turned his head just enough to break the kiss, Violet settled her weight on her knees to straighten and offer herself to him. Bronson dipped his head to kiss the hollow at her throat and inhale her scent again, but she closed her fingers at the back of his head and tugged him to her breast.

He molded her breasts in his hands and skimmed his closed lips over her curves. She was soft and warm, and Bronson was lost in the feel of her heat pressed against him.

She moaned softly in protest until he parted his lips to drop open-mouthed kisses over her soft skin.

"Bronson, please."

He inched lower and probed her nipple with the tip of his tongue. As if in the throes of an orgasm, Violet dropped her head back and moaned with appreciation. Fingers still clasped behind his head, she held him there at her breast. Only when he sucked her rosebud nipple into his mouth and worked it with his teeth did her grip loosen. The soft play of her fingers in his hair chased a shudder of pleasure down his chest and into his thighs.

Hungry for more of her skin, for more of her sweet, sexy sighs and moans, Bronson let his hands roam as he flattened her nipple to the roof of his mouth and then suckled her long and hard. The only sounds in her house the whisper of skin and clothing and their ragged breathing, he turned his attention to her other breast.

Violet drew away from him so suddenly, it startled him. Brain addled by lack of oxygen, he blinked her into focus and waited. Would she climb off his lap and ask him to leave? The mix of sex and vulnerability had every nerve in Bronson's body on alert. He wanted to fuck her; hell yes, he wanted to fuck her. But he wanted it to be everything to her, for her. His heart thundered with desire, with the need to lay her down and show her how intoxicating she was.

Something about her suggested that no one had ever done that.

She didn't climb off his lap. Rather, she reached for his shirt, fingers steady as she moved down the buttons. When she reached the last one, she tipped her head just enough to look him in the eyes and parted the shirt.

Bronson chuckled when she found his T-shirt beneath the button down, but Violet groaned softly.

"I need your skin." Her voice was thick and husky with

longing. He leaned forward to shrug out of the shirt, and Violet scrambled backwards off his lap.

"Violet." He cocked his head to study her when she reached for him.

"I want you to fuck me."

Her whisper was like a hard tug on his cock. He slipped out of the shirt as he stood, Violet's hands on the tail of his T-shirt before his arms were clear of the button-down. She pushed it up over his abdomen, but once his skin was bared, she abandoned the soft material and focused on him. Her smooth hands roamed over his stomach and then up over his chest. Bronson hooked his fingers in the collar and yanked the shirt over his head as she pressed her fingers into his shoulders, looking for purchase.

"Are you sure?" He took her hands in his and lifted them to his mouth, much the same as she had done to him only minutes before. Eyes on hers, he kissed her knuckles and waited for her to say yes.

"Yes." She nodded. "I want you in my bed."

Bronson captured her fingers in his lips and suckled. Violet swayed on her feet when he flicked his tongue over them. She tugged away from him, but just as quickly, she linked her fingers through his and turned away to lead him from the room.

He feasted on the lines of her bare back, the slight curve of her hips, the tight fit of the denim over her ass. In minutes, he would peel that denim away and replace it with his hands, his mouth. Reminded of her guardedness, of the sweet flirting they had done prior to tonight, Bronson felt a tiny flash of guilt at his lewd thoughts.

His fingers had done a number on her shag cut hair. She looked as if she'd spent hours in bed already with a man desperate to satisfy her. The contrast of her dark hair over the creamy pale skin of her neck and her shoulders made him hungry to bury his nose in the crook of her neck and sink his teeth into her shoulders and her toned upper arms.

Her bedroom was the second door down the short hallway. Bronson ignored the first door. He didn't want to see dolls or stuffed animals, anything that reminded him that the woman he was desperate to get naked, the woman he wanted to fuck, was a mother. As much as he wanted to get to know that woman, it could wait until tomorrow. At the moment, Bronson wanted to find heaven, and he had a good idea it was between Violet's legs.

She flipped a switch and flooded the room with soft, warm lamplight. Bronson's eyes were drawn to her bare back again, the sweet promise of curves and heat. Her bed was unmade, and the mental image of a naked Violet lying in the pale blue sheets made his already hard cock pulse against the fly of his jeans.

Before she could turn to him, he moved closer, swept her hair to the side, and dropped staccato kisses from her neck just under her ear to the delicate curve of her shoulder. She sighed with pleasure and lifted a hand to wrap her fingers around his neck. Bronson kissed the same path back to her ear and nipped at her earlobe. He wrapped his arms around her and smoothed his hands up her sides to play with her breasts. Violet leaned into him; the heat between their bodies a thrill.

"I've been thinking about this for a long time," he told her.

"Me, too."

"Do you lay in that bed and think about me and touch yourself?"

"Yes."

"Fuck." He dropped his hands to her hips and yanked her ass back to grind over his fly. "That's hot, Violet. That makes me so fucking hot for you."

Violet dipped her head forward. Bronson pushed her hair

over the other shoulder and explored her neck again. He inched his knuckles over her waistband and then slowly unbuttoned her jeans. She twerked her ass against him as he eased his fingers inside the denim to push them down.

"Faster, Bronson," she whispered. "Please."

"No." He abandoned the denim halfway down her hips and flattened his palms on her smooth belly.

"Please? I need you. I need this."

"Are you wet?" He rubbed his nose up her neck behind her ear. The soft brush of her hair tickled his face. Bronson felt the soft mewl in the back of her throat. With his palm still molded to her belly, he inched his fingertips under the waistband of her panties. Violet sagged against him and placed her hand over his.

He resisted her attempt to hurry him and only dipped his fingers low enough to feel the soft brush of her curls. He dragged his open mouth over her shoulder and sank his teeth in to nip her as he covered her breast with his free hand.

"Bronson!" His name slipped out on a sob when he pinched her nipple and pushed his other hand deeper into her panties. He grazed her clit with his fingertip but immediately moved his hand again to smooth over her belly.

"Every time I go home from a Wild Canyon party," his voice was rough and gravely, "I get off thinking about touching you like this."

"Please." She rested her head on his shoulder and turned her face to his. "Please touch me."

"I want my mouth here, Violet." He swept his fingers low over her clit again. "I wanna taste your pussy."

"Do it." She nodded. "Please. Do it."

With her jeans still around her hips and her panties still in place, Bronson pressed his finger to her clit and rubbed her in big, slow movements. With her head still on his shoulder, she squeezed her eyes closed and whimpered.

"Harder," she whispered. "Please."

He moved his finger and resisted her again when she tried to tug his hand back to where she wanted it. Bronson cupped her sex and nipped her shoulder again when he found her slick and wet. Violet tried to shift her feet when he slipped a finger inside her, but the denim limited her movement. Bronson added another finger and gently probed her folds.

"Do you like that?"

"Yes."

"But you want more?"

"Please?" she whispered with a quick nod.

This time, he withdrew his fingers from her slick heat and pressed them to her clit. He rubbed her core in the same big, slow movements, but when Violet moved with him to ride his hand, he pressed harder and faster for her. She groped for something to hold onto, curling her fingers around the bedpost and flattening her other hand on the wall by the bed.

She came hard, but she was quiet, biting off any screams or shouts and sinking her teeth into her lower lip. Her body quivered against his with the aftermath of the orgasm. Bronson moved quickly to remove her jeans and her panties and lowered himself to his knees behind her. He tipped his head back to take her in, hypnotized by her long lean legs and small hips. Ready to worship her again, Bronson touched her legs. He circled his fingers around her ankles and drew softly over her bare feet. Violet gushed a soft sigh and shivered.

"So beautiful," he whispered over the back of her knee. She trembled as he flicked his tongue over her skin, bathing the back of her knee and up her inner thigh.

"Bronson," she moaned. "Oh my God. More. Please."

Bronson skated his fingers over her thighs and turned his

mouth to her other leg, licking and tasting her, there, too. She gasped again when he sank his thumbs into her ass cheeks and spread her open. He nipped at her cheek and slipped his fingers between her legs again, brushing her swollen sex and drawing another whimper.

"Lie down," he commanded her. She looked at him over her shoulder, Bronson still on his knees. He nodded, lust knotting his stomach as she lifted a knee and then crawled up on the bed.

"I wanna see you," she whispered, eyes roaming over his bare chest and stopping at the waistband of his jeans. "Show me."

He had no intention of fucking her yet. He planned to spend time getting to know every inch of her body from her eyes to her toes with his hands and his tongue and his lips first. But if she wanted him naked, he wouldn't complain. She leaned back on her hands, her breasts high and proud, her eyes on his hands as he worked his jeans open and down over his hips. He kicked out of them, surprised when she moved to cup his cock through his boxer briefs.

"I want this." Her fingers danced over his cock and then smoothed up over his stomach. Bronson watched her trace the bit of dark hair that tapered down into his briefs. "I want you inside me."

"Not yet." He shook his head. He caught both her wrists in his hand and held her for a moment. "I'm gonna taste you, Violet. I'm gonna lick you and suck you into my mouth and make you come."

"Bron—"

"I wanna make you come unglued, Violet." He let go of her hands and pushed her hair from her face. "I wanna make you come so hard you scream." She swallowed hard as he lowered himself to his knees beside the bed.

"Do you like to do this?" she whispered uncertainly.

"Do I want to bury my face in your pussy and lap you up like cream?" He tipped his head to study her parted lips. She stared at him for a moment and finally nodded, but she dropped her gaze to the bed between them. Bronson watched her maul her lip with her teeth for just a second and then to save her from herself, he caught her chin in his hand and kissed her.

"Yes." His firm answer left no room for doubt. "I do."

"Because—"

"Do you not like it?" he asked gently.

She shrugged. "I'm not very good at it. I don't—"

"Why don't you relax and let me be good at it?" He kissed her, his lips on the corner of hers and then a trail of soft kisses over her cheek. "If you don't like it, I'll stop."

"It just…" She cleared her throat and shrugged, but she refused to meet his eyes. "Takes a long time…if…it happens at all."

Bronson traced his fingers down over her collarbone. He tweaked her nipple and then continued down to her belly button.

"What time will your daughter be home tomorrow?"

"Whenever I call Mom," she whispered softly.

"Then we have all night." He shrugged. She lifted her gaze to his. The wistful look in her eyes was a knife in his heart. "Trust me?"

She laughed softly. "Apparently, I do." She nodded. "I'm just…"

"Lay back and relax.," he directed her. She did, in small, jerking movements, but she kept her chin up to watch him as he slid his hands under her ass and pulled her to the edge of the bed.

"My ex didn't—"

"I'm not your ex, Violet," he reminded her. Fingers still curled under her ass, Bronson spread her open with his thumbs and pressed his open mouth over her. "And I love that you're letting me lick you like this."

Lust surged straight from his brain to his cock when she moaned and lifted her hips from the bed. Her ex-husband was a fool if he hadn't taken the time to learn what would drive Violet over the edge. His loss. Bronson sucked her sensitive skin into his mouth and grazed her with his teeth. She bucked against him and smoothed her hands over his head. Fingers inside her, he felt her pussy contract as she seized under him and called his name on a broken sob.

Spent, her arms fell away as he stood and stepped out of his briefs. Her eyes still glazed from the orgasm, she watched with interest as he plucked a condom from his wallet and rolled it over his cock. With her thighs spread wide, Violet reached for him as he lowered himself over her.

"Are you okay?" His whisper was gruff with need. After watching her come apart twice, hearing the moans and the way she'd called his name, Bronson was desperate to get inside her. But her uncertainty about oral sex, about her appeal to him, touched him.

She nodded.

"I'm...so...incredibly good." Her lips tipped up in a lazy smile. "I just want you inside me."

As if to prove her point, she wrapped her arms around him and dragged her fingernails over his sweat-slicked skin. She cupped his ass cheeks in her hands and arched her eyebrows expectantly.

Bronson eased into her with care, mindful of her comment earlier. Fourteen months. Since the divorce? Since she'd been with anyone? Violet watched his face with big eyes and shifted beneath him as he settled and stilled for a moment. Her slick folds were hot and tight around him. Teeth gritted and shoulders tense, Bronson counted to five to tamp down the fire in his veins.

"Perfect." He groaned through his clenched teeth. "Jesus, Violet, this is perfect."

She stroked one hand up his back to cup his head and lifted her head from the bed. Their lips met in a soft, intimate kiss, and Bronson moved over her. Slow and easy, to be gentle yes, but also to tantalize her and make her want more.

Violet moved with him; the vulnerable woman of minutes ago gone. She met him thrust for thrust and wrapped her legs around his waist to take him deep. Tongues and lips touching, dancing, over and over, until she tipped her head back and arched her back from the bed. Bronson pressed deeper and then held her when she shattered yet again. Gasping to breathe, she held onto him as she floated back to herself and Bronson picked up his pace to ride out his own release.

She moved when he slipped into the bathroom to dispose of the condom. When he returned, he found her curled up on her side in her sheets, with her head on her pillow. Hands on his hips, he dipped his head and studied her silently. Did she want him to stay? Or would she ask him to leave?

Rather than say anything, Violet simply smiled and patted the bed in invitation.

"Want me to lock up out there?" He nodded to the doorway. They'd left lights on, and he wasn't sure she'd locked the door after letting him in. She nodded and said please, her thick, husky voice turning him on again.

5

B ronson wouldn't have admitted it to anyone, especially to Violet—not yet—but he loved that she had invited him back to her bed after they made love. He checked the locks and turned out the lights, leaving their wine glasses and clothing strewn over the living room and went back to bed. Violet pressed into him immediately, all smooth skin and luscious curves. She lay with her head on his chest and her hand on his belly, and he judged from the way her breathing evened out, she slept. He wanted to, but sleep didn't always come easy for him. So, he simply closed his eyes and reveled in the feel of the woman in his arms.

He'd been with other women since Jillian. But none like Violet. None that stirred more than longing, more than his dick. He wasn't particularly proud of the string of women he'd had since Jillian, and there weren't that many. But he wasn't ashamed of the things he had done, either. He worked at the bar and grill; it was more than putting his time in. He enjoyed it. He loved the atmosphere; he liked being around people. Evenings with the flat screens tuned into NFL or MLB games, depending on the season. Local softball teams that came in to celebrate a win or drink off a loss. Guys that hit the bar for a beer before heading home from work. Women who came in for a night off from cooking and cleaning and homework. He lived for all of it, and occasionally, he met a woman he found attractive and interesting, and they hooked up.

Now and then, it lasted a week or two. Maybe a month. But he'd never found anyone to tempt him to go deeper. Not after Jillian had broken his heart.

Violet made him think things he hadn't for a very long time.

They made love twice before daylight pushed at the blinds on her windows. Bronson eventually slept, though not for long. When he woke up, and the clock on her nightstand read 7:12, he had a fleeting wish for coffee. Not just any coffee, but coffee with Violet. In her kitchen. With him in his jeans and her in nothing but his shirt. He doubted she would be open to it, especially since her daughter would be coming home. Even if her mother waited for Violet to call, it might be an awkward conversation if she called too late in the morning. He had no idea what sort of relationship she had with her mother, and though he wanted to know that and a million other things, he decided he should approach any hope of seeing her again with caution.

"It's morning already?" She buried her face in her pillow. Bronson, spooned behind her with her back to his chest, curled his hand around her hip and kissed the back of her neck.

"It is."

"Mmm." She stretched, her bare toes sliding over his shin, her foot stopping to rest over his. If she regretted the things they'd done together, she wouldn't do that, would she? She wouldn't rub her ass against his already hard cock. If she wished he weren't here, that he hadn't stayed the night, wouldn't she pull away from him? Send him packing?

"Good morning," he said when she pushed at him to scoot him over. She flopped on her back, leg still pressed to his, her foot over his.

"Good morning." She sounded sweet and sleepy, and Bronson wanted nothing more than to pull her close and hold her so she could sleep in. But the smile she offered him was small and hesitant, and though she wasn't panicking yet, he figured she was bound to ask him to go soon.

He couldn't just climb out of bed and leave her, though. He didn't want to smother her, to appear clingy. But he sure as hell didn't want her to think he was blowing her off as if their night together meant nothing to him.

She turned her head on her pillow to look at him and kissed him back eagerly when he dipped his head to kiss her. Her soft, warm lips took him right back into the darkness of the night, when she'd pressed hot, wet kisses down his chest to his belly and his hips and finally taken him in her mouth.

"No regrets?" His voice was a little gruffer than he would have liked. He could be careful not to hurt her and protect himself at the same time.

Another slow smile tipped her lips up, and she let her eyes roam over his face before meeting his again.

"No."

"Me neither," he promised her.

"Avery's just..." She cleared her throat and shook her head, her hair making a small scratching noise on her pillow-case. "She's too young. I need to be—"

"It's okay." Bronson rubbed his thumb over her lower lip before leaning in to drop another kiss there. "I get it."

Eyes locked with his, she simply nodded.

"I should go."

She nodded again, but neither of them rushed to move.

Bronson took another kiss, this one long and lingering. Her bare breasts too much to resist, he cupped them in his hand and tweaked her nipples one more time, and then climbed out of her bed. His balls and his dick throbbed with protest, but his brain won the fight. She had to call about her daughter, and more than likely, she would want to shower and pick up the house a bit before her little girl came home. Not to mention, if it had been over a year since she'd been with someone, she was going to be a bit tender after their night together. He didn't want to make it worse.

Bronson pulled his briefs and jeans on under her watch. He stepped into his loafers, surprised when she slipped from her bed to follow him when he left her room. She pulled the sheet from her bed and wrapped it around her breasts and stood watching while he tugged his T-shirt on and then shrugged his button-down shirt on.

"Can I see you again?" he asked when he was dressed and ready to leave.

"Of course." She nodded. "Frank makes sure I know about every party, even if I can't make them all."

Bronson studied her face, a sinking feeling tugging his stomach, his heart, down. He didn't want to wait for a party to see her again.

"Okay." He nodded and crossed the room to take her in his arms again. She held one arm close to keep the sheet pressed to her, but the other she threw around his back. He closed his eyes when she kissed his neck and then his cheek. "Can I call you?"

She tipped her head back to look at him and answered with a slow nod. "Yeah."

Again, she hadn't said no. She hadn't shut him down. But she hadn't reacted the way he hoped she would.

"Okay." He gave her another squeeze, surprised when she kissed him again.

"Thank you."

Those last whispered words followed him out to his car, but they weren't a comfort. Making love like they had, finding that level of intimacy and intensity, didn't call for a thank you. It wasn't like he had come to her and performed a service for her; he wanted to pursue a relationship with her.

He pulled away from the curb in front of her house with a headache and an empty sensation in his gut, worse than the way he felt nothing with the women he'd been with since Jillian. It hit him when he was halfway home that he didn't even know her last name.

———

PART OF BRONSON wanted to give into the childish urge to call Violet immediately, to get a feel for what she was thinking and where they stood. The other part of him—his adult brain—knew it was a bad idea. No matter what she was thinking, she needed time to process what they'd shared. She'd known when she invited him over the night before what she wanted from him. But Bronson wondered how long she'd been thinking that way about him, if she'd been as interested in him as early as he was tuned into her. Or if being surrounded by the sex at the parties had planted the idea in her head.

After a run and a shower, he felt more like himself. Less needy, though he most definitely wanted to talk to her again. He wanted to take her to dinner and a movie. To walk somewhere with her hand in hand. To watch the sunset or hold her in his arms while they danced. But he reminded himself to go easy, because he didn't want to spook her.

He lost himself behind the bar later in the evening. Watched football with the whole of the clientele in the bar but found himself drawn into conversations directly around the bar. He held his breath each time his phone buzzed, hoping he would find a message from Violet. But eventually, he decided she wasn't going to contact him over the weekend. Not when her daughter was around.

At midnight, when he closed the bar down, he noticed he did have a message on his phone. He didn't look closely, though, until he was out in his truck, alone. The message wasn't from Violet. It was Jillian.

Can I see you tonight?

6

B ronson wasn't up for dealing with Jillian tonight. He had all of Sunday to talk to her. In fact, maybe they could go out for lunch and catch up and then go their separate ways. He ignored her text, though, and planned to reply tomorrow.

Apparently, Jillian had other ideas. Bronson wasn't happy to find her Mini-Cooper in his driveway when he pulled in. At least she hadn't shown up at the bar and grill. The last thing he needed was for her to show up and involve herself in his life, his business, only to dredge up bad feelings and questions he didn't want to answer.

Jillian climbed out of her little car as he pulled his truck into the drive behind her. She looked good, but then, Jillian always looked good. Bronson kept his eyes on her as he hopped down from the truck and swung his door closed.

"I would have called you tomorrow, Jill," he said by way of greeting. "It's late."

Her gray wool coat nearly dwarfed her. When she shrugged, a jeweled pin on the lapel of the coat caught the moonlight and winked at him. Jillian offered him a hesitant smile as he approached her.

"I wanted to see you."

"How long have you been sitting in your car? It's cold out here."

"Donna told me you and Steve have the bar now. She said she thought you closed up at midnight, so I thought I'd take a chance that you'd be home soon."

"It's been a long day." He threw the words out, wishing Jillian would understand that he didn't want to get into anything heavy tonight.

"I miss you, Bronson," she said simply.

So much for waiting. He sighed and headed to the back door under the carport, Jillian on his heels. She stood back when he unlocked the door and then slipped inside without a word when he turned to usher her in. Bronson flipped on the kitchen light, tossed his keys on the counter, and fixed his gaze on his ex.

"I'm exhausted, Jill. Can't this wait for tomorrow? We could grab some lunch and catch up."

Hands in her pockets, she eyed him silently. Bronson grew uncomfortable under her gaze. What if she was naked under that coat? What if she'd come here for sex, and she was about to shrug the coat off to reveal skin and attempt to seduce him? He held his breath for a second, felt a little ache in his chest, and then sagged in relief when he noticed denim on her legs and ankle boots on her feet.

"We could do that," she said softly. "I'd love to catch up with you, Bronson. But it's not really why I came by tonight."

The slight arch in her eyebrows and the wistful expression on her face was a jab in his heart. He didn't want to hurt her, but he had no interest in anything she might be suggesting here in his home after midnight.

"Jill—"

"We could go to sleep together and wake up for breakfast together."

"I'm sorry, Jill, but I'm not interested."

"Since when have you been able to say no to me?" She stepped closer to him and reached for him. Bronson tried to back away from her, but with the counter at his back, he had nowhere to go. Jillian rested her hands on his chest, but she made no move to get closer.

"Maybe since you made your choice, and I wasn't it." He circled her wrists with his hands and lifted them from his chest. "Let me move my truck so you can get out."

"You really want me to leave?"

"I do." He nodded. "Let's meet for lunch tomorrow. Right now, I want to go to bed. Alone."

Jillian sighed. She backed away from him with a small nod.

"I guess I deserve that."

"It's not about what you deserve," he promised her. "I'm tired. I'm not interested in starting something with you right now."

"Okay." She tipped her head and offered him a sad smile. "I'll go. But I would like to see you tomorrow."

"Meet me at Fletcher's," he suggested. "Twelve-thirty."

When she agreed, Bronson grabbed his keys and led her back outside.

"Go home," he told her. "You shouldn't be out by yourself this late."

"I'm a big girl, Bronson," she reminded him. "I can take care of myself."

"Goodnight, Jill." He leaned over to drop a kiss on her cheek as he passed her to get in his truck and move it. Thankfully, she got in her car without argument and when Bronson backed into the street and idled there, she zipped out of the drive and drove off with a wave.

Once inside, relieved to have dodged that bullet but knowing Jillian wouldn't give up that easily, Bronson brushed his teeth and changed to athletic shorts to sleep in. He crawled into bed, his head and heart with Violet, wondering when he would see her again. It took a while for sleep to take him, but when it did, he was dead to the world for a solid six hours. He awoke surprised and a little disappointed that he hadn't dreamt about Violet, about the night they'd spent together.

After a crisp morning run, he showered and made coffee and then stood at his kitchen window wondering about her. They'd been together Friday night; he'd left her place yesterday morning. And he hadn't heard anything since then. His instinct was to call her, to check in on her. To flirt a bit, tell her he missed her. It's what he would have done before Jillian broke him down to the shell of the man he'd been when Violet had first walked into the Jacksons' parties. And before Friday night with Violet, Bronson thought it was the sort of thing she would want a man to do.

But he couldn't forget the way she'd thanked him yesterday before sending him on his way. Those words niggled in the back of his mind all damned day yesterday. They didn't sit well with him. What if Violet had just been looking for a hook up? No different from the parties, other than privacy. What if Bronson had scratched an itch for her, and now she was ready to move on?

He hated the indecisiveness. Hated that Jillian had done it to him, hated that he'd let her wreck him as he had. Armed with that frustration, he met his ex at Fletcher's with the beginnings of a headache and an impatient need to race through lunch. Once he set Jillian straight and let her know he had no desire to backslide into their relationship again, into the man he'd been with her, he would go home and call Violet.

Jillian saw him walk into the restaurant and waved him down from a table in the back. Thankfully, she was dressed in jeans and a cowl-neck sweater, no skin showing. Nothing to suggest that below the sweater, she wasn't wearing a bra. That she hoped to sweet talk him into leaving Fletcher's with her for a little afternoon fun.

"Hey." She hugged him when he approached. Bronson wrapped her in his arms and gave her a healthy squeeze, but he released her easily and nodded toward her chair. "I have to admit I was a little afraid you wouldn't show."

"I wouldn't do that, Jill." He pulled his own chair out to sit. "Not my style."

She answered with a small nod, her gaze moving quickly over his face and then to the window by their table.

"Still. Maybe I deserve it."

"I told you last night, it's nothing about what anyone deserves." He watched her struggle not to look at him, but he turned when their waitress appeared at the table. "Did you order, Jill?"

"Just a cup of your cheese soup," she mumbled with a quick glance at the young girl.

Bronson studied Jill for a moment, a little suspicious and a little worried, before ordering a burger and a Coke.

"Not hungry?" he asked when they were alone again.

Jillian shrugged and met his gaze again.

"What've you been up to? It's been a while." She flashed a smile—the one that used to light up the room for him. He waited—she was a pretty woman, and her smile was still gorgeous—but the room stayed the same, and his heart stayed right in his chest where it was supposed to be.

"It's been a few years," he corrected her. "Not sure we have time to cover all that ground."

"I have time," she said quietly.

"I don't."

"The bar? How's that going? Do you like it?"

Maybe if she'd have started with questions about his parents or the old neighborhood, he would have given her a quick answer, and they could be halfway through their conversation and out the door. But he loved everything about Ripcord—his bar, and he was touched that she chose to ask him about what he loved.

"I love it," he answered with a lazy, almost reluctant smile. "Steve Cooper and I run it together."

"That's what Donna said." Jillian fiddled with the ketchup bottle as she looked at him. "What in the world made you go from the bank to the food business?"

"You did," he admitted with a deep shrug. "And I'd say it's more about hospitality than food. I don't do the cooking. We wouldn't have been open a day if that were the case."

"How did I do that?" Her voice was no more than a thick whisper.

"I thought we were on the same page, and I thought we wanted the same things. And finding out that I was wrong…" He scrubbed his hand over his hair and sighed as he dropped it back to his lap. "I don't know, Jill. You left. And I decided it was time for a change. I could have stayed at the bank, and I could still be there. It was an okay job. But I wasted a few years of my life with that job. And…"

"And you wasted a few years of your life with me," she finished for him.

"They were good years, Jill, but," he shook his head, "yeah, I thought we were headed for more. I don't know what was worse. Finding out that you didn't want the same things I did or just realizing I read you that wrong."

"I'm sorry."

"Water under the bridge." He looked up when the waitress appeared again with his Coke, thanked her, and took a sip before putting the glass down.

"I wasn't ready."

"What're you doing now anyway?" He tipped his head and offered her a small smile. "Taking some part of the world by storm, I'm sure."

Jillian relaxed back in her chair with a startled laugh.

"Nope. No taking anything by storm these days." She pursed her lips. "I'm in human resources at a big construction company in southern Illinois."

"That sounds like something you would like." He grinned. "Jillian Keane working somewhere surrounded by men. Probably all rugged, sexy men, too, right?"

Once upon a time, the thought of Jill working around a bunch of guys anywhere—especially guys who might be muscular and rugged and sexy—would have made Bronson see red and spit nails. Now it filled him with regret that he hadn't been more in tune with what she wanted from life.

"No." She shook her head. "No, Bronson. I go to work. I do my job. I go home. No more wildlife. No more parties."

"Except Friday night," he reminded her.

"That's the first time I've done anything like that in over a year."

"Just like riding a bike?"

She chuckled, but he saw sadness flash over her face.

"I thought it would be fun."

"And?"

"It wasn't," she admitted. "I thought all this time I was missing the music and the drinking and the sex and the big life. Turns out, I was wrong."

"Tell me this." He tipped his head. "If you moved away to live that quiet life, why did you turn me down?"

"I didn't wanna get married," she said simply. "I had no interest in tying myself down and becoming a responsible adult and ending up pregnant and stifling who I am inside."

Bronson arched his eyebrows.

"But I did that anyway." Her voice was a whisper again. "I hated how I hurt you. I had to get away from that. From the guilt. From you."

He cleared his throat and looked around. "So, you came back to see your family, and you decided to hit up a party and get a fix."

"I came back to see you. And I ran into Donna, so she invited me to a party. Told me you were tending bar for her and Frank now."

"It's been interesting."

"I'm sure it has," she answered with a laugh. "I spent the evening playing cards with Frank."

Bronson frowned, disbelief making his head want to explode.

"I wanted to be with you, Bronson. No one else there."

Uncomfortable with the way she was watching him, Bronson squirmed a bit on his chair. Memories of the night he'd spent with Violet called to him. What would Violet think if she knew he'd proposed to Jillian a few years ago? Would it bother her if she knew he were with Jillian now? Or had he simply been a transition, a rebound hookup so she could move on?

"Is there someone else?" Jillian's gruff voice drew him out of his thoughts. He clenched his teeth together and pulled in a deep breath through his nose.

"I'd like there to be," he finally answered.

"She doesn't feel the same way?"

"I have no idea, Jill." He shrugged. "It's all pretty new."

"I don't wanna cause problems," she said quietly. "But I'm here. And you're here. And I want to spend time with you."

Bronson winced, but he said nothing.

"We were good together," she reminded him. "What if you still love me?"

"Oh, I do." He gave her a quick nod. "Always will. But I'm not in love with you, Jill."

Jillian sighed and tipped her head. "Gonna just love me like a friend for the rest of your life?"

"Something like that," he agreed.

"Forgive me, but if you're not sure about her, I'm gonna fight for you."

"I know how I feel about her. And I'll be fighting for her."

"Bronson."

"We had a shot at this." He shook his head. "And now we both have different lives."

"You could give me a second chance."

Shoulders tense, Bronson met Jillian's eyes. She arched her brows as if throwing down a challenge. He chuckled and shook his head again, but his phone buzzed in his pocket and sent his heart and head right back to Violet.

Violet's text sent a thrill through him that made him feel like a fourth grader with a crush on a favorite teacher. The text had only said *hey*, but she'd added a smiley face emoji. Bronson hadn't ever considered himself a sucker for emojis, but he couldn't deny even to himself that it hit him in the heart.

He'd answered Jillian on autopilot. Told her Violet was the woman's name, and when he'd glanced up at her from his phone—ridiculous that he couldn't tear his eyes away—he had seen the knowing look in her eyes.

"The woman at Donna and Frank's Friday night." She hadn't phrased it as a question, so Bronson hadn't bothered to answer. Instead, he texted Violet back. Just to say hi. Couldn't even bring himself to add a smiley face at this point, because even though he was relieved she had contacted him, he could still hear her thanking him when he left her house yesterday.

Jillian behaved through the remainder of the lunch date, although she did ask as they walked out together if Bronson had slept with her. When he refused to answer her, she only nodded. He wasn't sure if Jillian assumed he was involved with Violet or if she just understood that Bronson wasn't the type to kiss and tell.

Yet another reason why he had grown tired of the Wild Canyon Estates parties far quicker than Jillian.

When the evening rolled around and he hadn't heard from Violet again, he decided to call her. He waited until after seven, because he figured she and her daughter might be eating dinner or working on homework together. Hip hitched up at the counter, he wondered what her daughter— Avery—was like. Did she look like her mother? Or like Violet's ex-husband? Would the girl be open to her mom having someone new in her life? Had Violet's ex cheated? Was he remarried?

They hadn't covered any of that. Maybe they hadn't talked enough, but when she kissed him, he had known they both needed the intimacy. The *physical* intimacy. Bronson still wondered if Violet had been divorced for fourteen months, or if she meant she hadn't been with anyone for fourteen months. If any warm body on her couch would have filled her need or if she was as interested *in him* as he was her.

"Hey." Her soft, warm voice in his ear chased a shiver up his spine. "I was hoping you would call."

"You were?"

"Mmm." She cleared her throat. "Hang on one second."

"Okay."

He listened as she spoke with her daughter. Her voice was muffled, as if she had tilted the phone away from her face, but he heard her tell Avery she had thirty minutes of TV time and that she would be in the kitchen if Avery needed her.

Bronson imagined Avery in the living room. Maybe

sprawled on the floor, with her chin in her hand, eyes on some kind of kid friendly programming. He couldn't picture her on the couch, not when he was still thinking about Violet straddling his lap and leaning in to steal kisses from him.

Steal, hell. He'd give her everything, every damned day of the week.

"Sorry." Her voice was back now, soft but clear. "I wish you were here."

"That could be difficult," he said with a grin. "I'm assuming she's watching TV in the living room, and I'm thinking about undressing her mother there on the couch."

The sound from her end of the phone—a soft moan of intense longing—rendered him speechless for a moment.

"I thought about you last night," she whispered.

"You did?" He lowered himself to his own sofa and kicked back to revel in her words.

"Yes."

"And what were you thinking about?"

"The way you felt inside me."

"Can she hear you?"

"No." She cleared her throat. "I'm sorry." She trilled a nervous little laugh. "God, I probably sound desperate, don't I?"

"You sound sexy as fuck." He lowered his hand to his fly to adjust his dick. The denim he'd been wearing comfortably all day was suddenly a bit tight.

"Do you think so?"

"I can't get you outta my head," he admitted. "Your hair on your bare shoulders. You spread out naked on your sheets. The way you taste."

She whimpered softly. "That's not fair."

"Can I see you again?"

"Yes."

"When?"

"Tomorrow."

"My bar's closed on Mondays," he told her.

"I could bring dinner by after I leave work."

"What about your daughter?"

"She has a scout troop meeting after school. She'll go home with a friend, and I get her after work. I'll let Cindy know I might be a bit late picking her up."

. So, their time together would be limited. He didn't like the sound of that. And yet, it was better than nothing. Until Violet trusted him to be around her daughter, he would have to take what she was willing to give him.

"I'm looking forward to it."

―――――

BRONSON REFUSED to sit around all evening and think about Violet and what would happen when he would see her Monday after she left work. He liked her, but he'd had his heart broken and he'd changed as a result of that relationship. He would proceed with caution as far as Violet went, and maybe their fling would become more. Maybe not. He wasn't ready to throw everything into pursuing her just yet.

Instead of worrying about her and what she'd meant when she thanked him Saturday morning, he twisted the top off a bottled beer and kicked back in his recliner to watch a movie. Channel-surfed when the movie bored him and found himself drawn into a documentary on jazz musicians.

Monday morning brought thoughts of Violet, but again, Bronson refused to let the uncertainty overwhelm him. He went for a run and then hit his home gym for some weightlifting. He'd always been somewhat health conscious, but the workouts and the running had been something he

picked up after splitting up with Jillian. A lot of people
assumed the fitness was about vanity—maybe rightly so,
considering he spent a lot of time at Frank and Donna Jackson's house and bodies were always on display there.
However, Bronson didn't point out to them that as the
bartender, he tended to keep his clothes on, and he didn't
admit to anyone other than himself that the fitness routine
was as much about mental health as it was physical.

Pushing himself to his physical limits had been his best
coping method when he had proposed to Jillian and she
turned him down. Walked out on him and the relationship
he had thought was forever. He'd come close to confessing as
much to Donna once, but he'd held the words in. Bronson
suspected that she knew what he was thinking, feeling,
without him saying the words. Which only made him
wonder why she hadn't told him Jillian was back in town.

After a hot shower and coffee and eggs, Bronson decided
it was a good day to winterize the house and the yard. The
cold, brisk air kept him moving as he checked the windows
and screens and found them all in good shape. The house
he'd grown up in was old, and the caulking on the windows
had to be redone every few years to keep the drafts out. His
dad had been a hard worker, always one step ahead of the
responsibilities of a homeowner. The house wasn't a castle,
but he'd made it as perfect as he could for Bronson and
his mom.

He supposed his parents had set a good example for him
all the way around. Not only were they hard workers—as a
popular seamstress, his mom was always busy—they loved
each other. Always. Not to say Bronson hadn't witnessed
fights, but somehow even during the worst of the fights, as a
kid, Bronson had still understood they loved each other.
They were friends, too. Bronson had always liked that his
parents chose to do everything together, rather than finding

hobbies that pulled them apart, like so many of his friends' parents did.

As a teenager, even into college, Bronson had been a partier. In the back of his mind, he knew that he wanted the same sort of relationship his parents had. One day. But he wasn't in a hurry to be a responsible grown up. He trusted that one day he'd be ready to settle down, and he would find someone he wanted to spend the rest of his life with. Someone he wanted to have kids with.

For a while, he thought Jillian was that woman.

As much as he wanted to paint himself into Violet's family now, he knew the best way—the only way—to proceed was with patience and a level head.

Bronson was just about finished cleaning the garage out when Violet pulled an older model Civic into his short drive. From the back of the garage, he turned and watched her climb out of the car and then lean in to grab a brown paper bag. Hands propped on his hips, he watched with interest. Part of him had wondered if picking up dinner had been a euphemism for coming over for sex. He still wasn't sure how he felt about dinner or sex; given his choice, he would ask for both. Dinner, so they could have face time. Talk to each other more. Damn right, Bronson wanted to take Violet to bed again, but he wanted to know her better. He had been drawn to her voice, her laughter, just from talking to her at Frank and Donna's parties. He wanted more of that, more of her charm and her personality, just as much as he wanted more of her hot mouth and soft, small curves.

The carport hadn't been in terrible shape to begin with, because—as Jillian used to tease—Bronson was a bit over the top with cleanliness. But Bronson was still sweaty, and he figured he had dirt streaked over his face or arms or something as he eyed his toolbox one more time and then, satisfied that every screw driver and wrench was in the proper place, he closed the drawer and headed out to greet Violet.

"Hi." She stopped short at the entrance to the carport and eyed him uncertainly. She held the brown paper bag up in offering, the smile she offered him making her eyes twinkle. Bronson groaned softly when she dragged her teeth over her lower lip. He felt the touch low on his abdomen, where Violet had licked his hot skin before taking his cock in her mouth.

"Hi." He took the bag from her, but instead of opening it, he lifted it and sniffed the air to guess what she'd brought. He tipped his head at her and narrowed his eyes. "Barbeque?"

"That okay?" she asked with a nod.

Yes, he wanted to sit with her and share a meal. But she dragged her eyes down over his chest and his waist, making him decide he wouldn't care if she offered him mud pies for dinner.

"That's perfect." He reached for her hand, a jolt of electricity zipping up his arm to his neck when she linked her fingers with his.

"What were you doing?" She looked around his carport as she followed him to the door.

"Straightening things up," he told her. "I mowed the yard. I assume it'll be the last time this year."

"It's supposed to snow this week."

"And do you like snow?" He led her into his small kitchen and set the bag on the counter. "Beer?"

"I like beer, and I'm undecided on snow."

"Undecided?" He shot her a look as he pulled the refrigerator door open and grabbed two longnecks.

"I don't love it, but Avery does," she explained. "If I'm with Avery, I love it."

Bronson nodded as he twisted the tops off the bottles and handed her one.

"I get that."

"She loves to make snow angels."

"And do you?"

"No." Violet laughed softly. "I've got nothing against snowmen, but snow angels." She shook her head with a severe frown.

"You have a thing against angels?"

"No. Just don't love rolling around in snow. No matter if I'm wearing a big coat, I always end up with snow on my back. What's to love about that?"

Bronson arched an eyebrow and pretended to consider her question.

"Does Avery like to go sledding?"

"She does." Violet tipped the bottle for a drink.

"Maybe we could all go this year. If we get the right kind of snow."

He didn't know what got into him. Shouldn't have suggested it. It was one thing to ask to see Violet again, but it was completely different to suggest that she would be okay introducing him to her daughter.

Violet set her bottle down. She looked back at him with a small smile. Bronson shifted on his feet as she stepped closer to him and rested her hands on his chest.

"She would like that," she agreed. "If we get the right kind of snow."

"Where do you work?" He ran his hands over her arms, his eyes roaming over her silver blouse and black slacks.

"V." She grinned a little self-consciously. "I'm Dr. Cronin's assistant."

"V. The Vision Clinic?"

"Yep." She licked her lips. "I didn't think I had time to go home and change before coming by."

"Why would you?" He leaned in to kiss her cheek. "Office professional is very sexy on you."

Violet dipped her head back and laughed softly. "Right. Nothing says middle-aged and divorced like office professional attire."

"Do you like what you do?"

"I do." She nodded.

Bronson flicked her lips with the tip of his tongue. "Then it's very sexy."

Violet parted her lips in invitation and kissed him back with hunger that matched his own.

"I…" She broke the kiss to speak, but only managed a shaky sigh when he licked a trail down her neck. "Bought us more time."

"What do you mean?" He drew back and studied her face closely.

"My mom's picking Avery up from her friend's." Her voice dropped to a whisper, as if she wasn't sure Bronson would be happy with the news.

"Yeah?" He grinned. "So we can have dinner and dessert?"

"If you want me to stay for a while."

"If I—" He gave himself a mental shake. "Oh, I do, Violet. But first things first."

"Dinner?" She nibbled on her lip again.

"Oh, no." He reached for the button of her slacks and opened it with a quick twist. "First, I'm going to eat you. I've been hungry to taste you again since the second I walked out of your house Saturday."

"Bronson." She laughed softly, as if she were going to object. But she obediently stepped out of her slacks when he slid them down her legs, and they pooled at her feet. She started to step out of the small black kitten heels, but he shook his head and unbuttoned the bottom three buttons on her blouse.

"This is fucking perfect," he told her. "Just like this."

She watched with wide eyes when he hooked his thumbs

in her panties and eased them over her hips. Bronson heard her gasp when she latched onto his shoulders. He slipped his arms around her waist and cupped her ass cheeks in his hands to lift her. She fluttered her feet and kicked the scrap of silk out of the way and then wound her legs around him.

"I've been thinking about your bedroom," she whispered.

"We're not going to my bedroom."

"We're not?"

"Not yet." He ducked his head and nibbled on her earlobe. Bronson took three steps and eased her onto the small counter on the east wall of his kitchen.

"Here?" She whispered with a giggle. "Really?"

"Can't think of anything I'd rather eat right here in my kitchen." He nodded. Violet rocked back gently to lean on the silver backsplash tile on the wall. Bronson parted her legs and pushed gently at her inner thighs until she was completely bared to him.

"Are you wet?" he asked her.

A smirk her only answer, Bronson dipped his eyes over her blouse, now hanging open over her flat belly. The button over her breasts was still closed; the glimpse of her skin as much of a thrill to him as her wet pussy.

"Would you do this to me at a party?"

"Lick you? Suck you? Until you come?"

"On the bar."

"Fuck." Bronson sucked in a quick breath. "I'd do it to you anywhere you want it, Violet. A hundred times a day."

"With other people watching?"

"If that's what you wanted."

He felt her eyes on him as he traced his fingertips over her inner thighs and then rubbed his thumb up over her clit.

"Have you ever?"

"Ever what?" He flicked his eyes up to meet hers for a second, but he had to look again at the lips of her sex. He eased his finger inside her, careful to stroke inside her the way she'd liked it the other night.

"Given someone oral sex on the bar at a party?"

"Not on the bar." He shook his head. "Because that would probably be a health code violation."

The low rumble of laughter that rolled up from her belly zapped his dick.

"I fucked myself with my vibrator last night," she told him, her voice thick with lust. "And thought about you."

"Yeah?" He continued to pump his fingers into her and slide them out with care to make her crazy. "Did you come?"

She nodded.

"Was it as good as being with me?"

"No."

"Good." He tipped his head and narrowed his eyes at her. "Because as much as I fucking love that you've been fantasizing about me, I want you to need me."

"Bronson." She lifted her hips from the counter and covered his hand with hers.

"Nope." He withdrew his fingers and licked them, eyes locked with hers. "I'm gonna fuck you with my mouth, Violet."

"Please?"

"Touch your breasts."

Without breaking eye contact, Violet reached for the last button of her blouse.

"Leave it buttoned. Push your bra out of the way."

"Is this hot?" She eyed herself as she did as he demanded. Bronson's gaze lingered on her hands, filled with her breasts, the silver silk draped over her.

"You are so fucking hot, I'm gonna come just putting my mouth on you."

"Bronson."

He watched her play with her breasts, a little bit sorry

now that he hadn't demanded that she take her blouse off. It was sexy, knowing what she was doing to herself under the blouse, but he wanted to see her curves, her pink nipples hard and ruby red with excitement.

His cock ready to explode already, Bronson pushed her thighs open again and ducked his head between her legs. He stroked his nose over her clit, the smell of her arousal turning him on more. She whimpered when he nudged the sensitive skin with his tongue.

"Fuck me." Her whisper was harsh and desperate.

Bronson wrapped his fingers around her outer thighs and yanked her forward as he plunged his tongue into her hot, wet folds. He licked her walls and dragged his teeth over her clit, sucking her hard into his mouth, only to flick her clit again with his tongue.

Violet's legs draped over his shoulders; he felt her heels in his back. She moaned as she rocked her hips to fuck his face.

"Are you touching yourself?" he managed to ask before sliding his tongue deep inside her again.

"Yes."

"Tell me. What're you doing?"

"Pinching my nipples." The words gushed out, her voice vibrating with pleasure and pain. "I want you to touch me. To bite them."

"I will," he promised her.

"Bronson, I'm gonna come."

"Come for me, Vi. Come hard. I wanna feel you gush all over my face."

"I'm coming...feels so fucking good, Bronson," she sobbed. She panted hard as he worked her with his mouth. He felt her hands moving over his head and wished for a second that he could pull away and watch her work her nipples. But she was so close, and he wanted to push her over the edge.

Finally, she yelped and called his name. Her fingers smoothed over his head, and he tasted her release on his tongue and his lips.

"Stay," he whispered. "For a while. Please stay for a while?"

8

"What'd you tell your mom?" Bronson took a bite of his sandwich—Violet brought a pulled pork and a pulled chicken sandwich and told him to choose. He'd taken the pork, though he would have eaten either.

"Hmm?" She licked her lips and then laughing, she covered her mouth with her hand, to chew her own mouthful. Still on the counter, though she'd let her legs dangle, she reached for her beer and held the bottle as she watched Bronson.

Because she was wearing silk and eating barbeque, Bronson had suggested she might like to take her blouse off. The faint blush in her cheeks had chased a rush of blood straight to his dick, but she'd offered him a small smile and told him he was right. Bronson had unwrapped his own sandwich, eyes on her as she shrugged the silk off and tossed it aside. He had considered suggesting she take her bra off, because that could be messy, too. In the end, he hadn't said it, but she had taken a look down at herself—sitting on his kitchen counter wearing only a white lace bra—and shrugged. Bronson's dick had throbbed when she reached back to unhook the material and shrugged it off, too.

"This okay?" She'd tilted her head and offered him a flirty grin. "Naked woman sitting on your counter to eat dinner?"

"More than okay," he'd answered with a nod.

"You do this often?" she asked now, waving the hand holding her sandwich at him. Bronson, still fully dressed, stood at her side, hip resting on the counter.

"Do what often?"

"Eat barbeque while standing fully clothed and stare at the nude woman on your counter? Who's also eating barbeque?"

He laughed softly.

"I have never done this in my life."

"Interesting," she murmured after studying him for a moment.

"How so?"

She shrugged and shook her head as if emerging from a daydream.

"I'm guessing you've got stories, Bronson Hart. Some incredibly sexy stories. Hard to imagine you haven't had naked dinners before."

"Didn't say I haven't had naked dinners," he clarified. "But none quite like this."

Violet took a sip of her beer. "Is that good?"

"Damn straight, it is." He nodded.

"'kay."

"You didn't answer me," he reminded her.

"What?"

"What did you tell your mom? When you asked her to pick up Avery?"

Violet grinned and nibbled on her sandwich again. "You mean, did I tell her I was coming over here?"

He shrugged, but he gave in a with a nod and a curious frown.

"I told her I met someone," she admitted. "I sort of mentioned you a long time ago."

"Really?" He polished off his sandwich and then wiped his hands and mouth on a napkin.

"Told her I was talking to someone at a party."

"Yeah?" Bronson felt his lips twitch.

"I didn't tell her anything else about the parties, because she would totally come unglued." Violet laughed softly. "I know I'm an adult, but I don't know a lot of adults who get into that sort of thing. My mom certainly wouldn't understand."

"I get it." He raised his eyebrows and then stepped to the sink to wash his hands.

"Um, so yeah. I just told her that you and I had spent some time together the other night, and that we were going to have dinner together."

Bronson balled the paper bag up and tossed it in the garbage. He gave her the side eye as he did so.

"You didn't tell her that you were coming over for sex?"

"This isn't just sex, Bronson," she mumbled, eyes big with wonder. This time, it was Bronson's heart that felt her words.

"No?"

"This is the best fucking sex I've ever had." She laughed a bit self-consciously. "I thought I had a good sex life with…my ex. I mean, he was…" She licked her lips. "I was wet all day at work thinking about you. The way you look at me. The way you say my name when you're licking me."

Bronson adjusted his dick and turned to her, aroused again but disappointed, too.

"Can I fuck you right now?"

Violet bit her lip, but she put the remainder of her sandwich on the counter.

"I need to brush my teeth."

He stepped toward her and brushed the back of his knuckles over her nipple.

"That's not fair."

"You can use my toothbrush," he offered. "And I'll show you my bedroom."

"You don't care if I use your toothbrush?"

"Not if it means I get to fuck you."

Violet flashed him a grin as she slipped off the counter and scooted down his body. Feet on the floor, she looked up at him. Bronson pressed into her, loving the flush in her face when she felt his cock hard against her middle.

"Maybe I need dessert." She pursed her lips.

"I need you on your back with your legs open." He pushed her hair back from her face. "Because I need to bury this inside you."

He caught her hand and set it over his fly.

Violet's eyes darkened with lust as she cupped him.

"Let me suck you off."

Before he could protest, she had his jeans pushed open and her hand in his briefs. Her knowing fingers curled around his shaft and stroked gently.

"Bedroom," he insisted.

"Lead the way."

Their bottles still half full on the counter, Bronson led her by the hand up the steps to his bedroom at the left. He had turned the spare room into his home gym, and while the thought of fucking her in there, in front of the mirror, excited him, right now, he simply wanted her in his bed.

At his bed, though, Violet pushed his jeans over his hips and freed his cock. Against his will, he rocked into her hand, hungry for her attention.

"Violet," he groaned as she sank to her knees in front of him. "I wanna get inside you."

"Okay." Her breath was hot over his skin. She skated soft kisses over his thighs and traced his shaft with her tongue. Bronson tipped his chin to watch her as she closed her lips around the head of his cock. He pushed her hair from her face and met her eyes when she looked up at him, but he shook his head and urged her back to her feet.

"If we have a time limit together, I want to make love to you." His voice was gruff with honest emotion. Violet didn't seem to notice his word choice; she sank her teeth into his collarbone and wrapped her arms around his waist. Bronson turned her around to lay her down on his bed and reached for the drawer of his nightstand.

————

THEY DIDN'T TALK. He didn't ask her about the divorce, about her ex. She didn't offer personal information. In the heat of the moment, he didn't care. He decided they would talk later, but later, after another hour of rolling around in his bed together—touching and kissing—Violet kissed his cheek, announced she had to get going, and slipped out of his bed.

"You wanna take a quick shower?" he offered, hungry eyes roaming over her nude body at the foot of his bed. "Before you pick Avery up?"

Violet grinned. "She probably wouldn't notice, but Mom might."

Bronson laughed as he rolled out of bed and nodded for Violet to follow him to the bathroom down the hall. He grabbed linens from the closet and set them on the counter.

"I don't have any soap that smells half as good as you do." He shrugged, feeling like he won the lottery when she laughed softly. "But you're welcome to whatever you need in here."

"Thank you." She nodded.

Bronson turned to walk out of the room and give her privacy, but the look in her eyes drew him back to her. He stepped closer and lifted a hand to cup her chin.

"I wish you could stay," he said quietly.

"It's just...with it being a weeknight...and Avery has school tomorrow—"

"I know." He smoothed his thumb over her lip and then leaned in close to kiss her. "I get it. But I want you to know where I'm at here. And I would love it if you could just spend the night in my bed. I'd love to wake up with you in my arms."

Violet pressed her lips together and laughed when he moved back, letting his fingers trail down her neck and over her breast.

"Me, too."

"I'll bring your clothes up for you," he said as he stepped out of the room and pulled the door closed behind him. Because the thought of walking back into the bathroom and joining her in the shower was too appealing, Bronson returned to his bedroom and pulled on the jeans Violet had removed from his body earlier. He took a moment to study his bed—the sheets were twisted and loose, so he would just pull them off and throw them in the washer after Violet left —and imagined the two of them there together again.

He hurried back downstairs and gathered her clothes and then took them back to his bedroom. If he put them in the bathroom with her, he would still be tempted to shuck his jeans and climb into the shower with her. Seemed like a good idea—his dick thought so—but he wanted more than steamy sex, and as much as he wanted Violet to stay with him, he knew she needed to get home to her daughter.

Her hair was still messy when she joined him in the kitchen again, as if she hadn't washed it but simply tousled it with her fingers. She buttoned the last button of her blouse as she appeared in the room with him and then dropped her hands to her sides. Bronson, in the midst of cleaning the remains of their dinner mess, shot her a grin from across the room.

"Let me pay you for the sandwiches," he offered.

"Nope." She shook her head and looked around for her purse and keys. "You get the next one."

"Next one?" He wagged his eyebrows at her and moved to stand by her. "You wanna see me again?"

"I do." She rested her hands on his shoulders and tipped her head back to watch him through narrowed eyes. "Is that okay?"

"Yes."

"I would love to come back tomorrow," she whispered. "But…"

"I know." He slipped his arms around her waist. "As much as I want to see you again, I don't want to keep you from your daughter."

"Most guys wouldn't get that." She lowered her gaze and watched her thumb as she swept it over his chest. Bronson waited to see if she met his eyes again. When she didn't, he eased closer and kissed her forehead.

"I'm not most guys," he said simply.

"Maybe Friday?" She finally flicked her gaze up to meet his, but she looked away quickly.

"Definitely."

She nodded. "Avery stays with my mom one night every weekend."

"Okay." Bronson smoothed his hands low over her ass and gave her a quick pat. "What about dinner first?"

Violet laughed softly.

"Like we had dinner tonight?" Her cheeks flushed a bright red.

"You like that, don't you?" He rested his chin on her head. "My face between your legs."

"I love that," she confessed. "Kody didn't have the patience for it."

Bronson stiffened at her ex's name. Yes, he wanted to know what happened that caused their split. In the most general sense. If she was still hurt. If she still loved him. But he had no desire to hear about her ex-husband's bedroom skills or lack of.

"Maybe Kody wasn't doing it right," he suggested, "because any time I kiss you there, you're so sensitive and so aroused, you come fast and hard."

"Is that okay? Do I come too fast?"

"Are you kidding me?" He drew back to look at her, surprised to see the uncertainty on her face. "It's hot as fuck and only makes me want to do it again. And again. And again."

She gave him a hesitant smile and then nodded, but she looked away. "He always said I was good...that I gave good head, and he could make me come with his fingers, so that should be enough."

Bronson flinched. "Well, he was wrong. I will go down on you every chance I get, Violet."

She shivered and pressed herself against him.

"You're incredible, Bronson." She kissed his bare chest.

"One question."

"Hmm?"

"I don't even know your last name."

Her warm breath fanned over his chest when she laughed softly. "Clayton. Violet Clayton."

"Okay. Well, Violet Clayton, on Friday, I would like to take you out for dinner. On a date. And then take you home. And I'd be happy to strip you down and eat you for dessert and then take you to bed."

She groaned and rolled her forehead on his chest.

"Now I don't wanna leave."

"Go." He kissed the top of her head again and then dropped his hands to his sides. "Before I pick you up and take you back upstairs."

9

They texted often before Friday, and they spent some time on phone calls. But Bronson tried to be respectful of her time with Avery. He figured it would suck for a seven-year-old girl to sit and watch her mom talk on the phone all the time, even if they weren't talking dirty. He found himself thinking of Violet all the time and tried to remind himself to slow down. Just because she was into him in bed didn't mean they had a future. It was entirely possible that she hadn't been with anyone at all since she'd been divorced, and she was just venturing back into that world. In fact, odds were that was the case. Violet was a parent, so Bronson assumed she had taken the past year to care for her daughter, to make sure she was okay.

Bronson might be her rebound guy.

He was a bit old to be a boy toy but based on the things Violet had said to him, it was entirely possible that she was using him for sex. He didn't want to believe that, but the thought nagged at him every day. There were worse things, he supposed. Sex with Violet certainly wasn't a hardship. But he would be kidding himself to think he would be satisfied if that was all that came of the time he'd spent with her.

On Friday, dressed in khakis and a white button-down shirt, he knocked on her door with his heart in his throat. He hadn't been on a date in years, not since Jillian. After that heartbreak, he'd taken his turn using women for sex. He'd always made sure they understood that of him, though. He hadn't wanted to lead any woman on, not after the way Jillian had hurt him.

It surprised him that he was nervous. He'd never thought of himself as a ladies' man, but he'd never doubted himself with women, either. Jillian had crushed him, and sure, he'd stopped trusting anyone with his heart. But he'd never doubted that women found him attractive and fun. He'd never doubted himself as a lover; he'd delivered with Jillian and the other women he'd been with.

But a date? Picking a woman up and taking her out somewhere to show her a good time? To share conversation? That was completely different. His heart almost exploded out of him when the door opened suddenly. He grinned--amused at himself and thrilled to see her—as their eyes met. Her painted on jeans left nothing to the imagination. Bronson swept his eyes down over her in an appreciative study and nodded his approval. The red blouse, open at the collar, made her dark eyes pop. She'd twisted her hair into a messy knot at the back of her head, and all Bronson could think about was later, when he would pull the clip from her hair and watch it fall over her naked shoulders as he moved down her body to put his mouth on her.

"Ready?" He cleared his throat. He hoped she couldn't see his erection now. Standing on her front porch, ready to take her to dinner, his dick decided it was ready to take her clothes off her and fuck her speechless and to hell with dinner.

"Yeah. Let me grab my jacket." She nodded and turned her back to him. Bronson propped his shoulder against the doorframe as she snatched a black leather jacket from the back of the recliner. She grabbed her purse, too, and then turned back to him with a sweet smile.

"You look incredible," he told her. "Red is definitely your color."

"Really?" She looked at him and arched her brows as she flipped the light switch and pulled the door closed. Bronson helped her with the jacket and then draped his arm around her shoulders as he steered her down the walk to his truck.

"Mm-hmm." He nodded. "I mean, I might like you best in nothing at all. Maybe in my sheets." He tipped his head back and forth, as if considering, and then flashed her a grin. "But you look beautiful."

"Thank you." She nodded up at him when they stopped at the passenger door. "I missed you."

"Did you?" He hooked his fingers in her belt loop and tugged her closer.

"I keep dreaming about being with you," she whispered. "The things you do to me."

"Like what?"

She blushed and tried to catch her breath. "That spot you kiss on the back of my shoulder. And the way you hold my breasts in your hands when we just lie together."

"I miss the feel of your hair on my chest when we lie together," he told her.

He kissed her, tempted to linger when she parted her lips.

"Nope." He laughed and backed away. "I am taking you to dinner."

"Where are we going?"

Bronson pulled her door open and waited for her to climb in.

"Rupert's," he told her. "Been there?"

"No."

He swung her door closed and then hurried around the front of the vehicle.

"Steak and seafood." He climbed into the driver's seat and looked at her as he started the truck. "That okay?"

"Perfect." She nodded.

"Good." He backed out of the drive and headed west. "Was Avery excited about going to your mom's?"

"She was," Violet answered with a smile. "They play Scrabble."

"Wow."

"Ave reads really well for her age. So, she's good at the game, and it's good for her."

"Did you tell your mom you had a date?"

"Told Mom," Violet said quietly. "But not Avery."

"Would she be upset?"

"I don't know."

"Tell me about your ex."

"What?"

Bronson spared her a glance as he navigated the streets of Rockfield. "All I know about him is that you said he tries to be a good dad to Avery, but he sucked at oral sex."

Violet snorted and rolled her eyes.

"Wait. I'll rephrase. He sounds like a selfish lover."

"You really wanna talk about him?"

"No. I don't really wanna know anything about the things you did with him." He shrugged and winked at her. "I guess I'm asking what happened."

"Why we're divorced."

"Is it okay? If I ask?"

"Of course," she mumbled. "He didn't cheat. If that's what you're thinking."

"Okay."

"I don't know. Lots of little things. That piled up and

seemed big. Most of our fights were about money. Kody liked to spend. I don't know if he wanted his friends to think we had a lot, but he was generous with them. To a fault. He was a big tipper. He liked to outdo himself with gifts for his friends' kids, and he liked to treat them when we went out. All great, but he ended up losing his job. He's an engineer, worked for a firm that made elevators. They downsized."

"Were you working then?"

"Yeah. And I loved the job. But it's hard to support a family like that. And then, he had the crazy idea to start gambling little bits here and there. I don't know if he thought he could eventually win real money. If that's how it started. If he just decided it was more fun to sit at the bars and bet on sporting events and horse races and every damned thing out there. He played poker. He started playing slot machines. He was losing money right and left. I told him he had to choose. That life or me and Ave."

"And he chose that scene over you?"

"He said he would do better. He did. For a week, maybe. And then, he was right back at it. So, I filed for divorce. It was ugly, Bronson. That all sounds very simple, and maybe you think I overreacted. But it was hard. He was hurting her. Forgetting things he promised her. Breaking promises."

"I'm not judging you, Violet," Bronson assured her.

"She was four when it started."

"Wow."

"He's been better about seeing her. I know he would never hurt her intentionally. They go fishing a lot when they're together. Avery loves it."

Bronson eyed her intently for a moment before turning his attention back to the road. He slowed and pulled into the lot at the side of Rupert's. They walked in companionable silence through the crowded lot; Bronson reached for her hand, surprised that she was so cold. He pressed her fingers between his hands and rubbed vigorously before letting go to pull the door open for her.

Inside, the sounds were hushed, and the lighting low and atmospheric. Rupert's was a small local joint with limited seating. Bronson knew Rupert Michaels personally and enjoyed his place. He had asked for a table with privacy when he called for reservations, but there were no bad seats here. Still, he was relieved when the host led them to a table for two near the back of the trendy place.

"Wine?" Bronson asked her when they were seated.

"Yes."

"Do you like seafood?"

"I do."

"Can't beat their lobster. The scallops are always good. Crab legs are good. But their steaks are excellent, too."

Violet grinned and tipped her chin to her chest. Bronson watched her study the menu.

"What?"

"I don't know how I'm going to eat," she said honestly. "Because all I can think about is how good it's going to feel when we go back to the house and make love."

Bronson felt her words like a sharp jab in his gut.

"I can't wait for that," he spoke in a small, tight voice, and tried to control the ridiculous grin on his face. "But. We have all night, and I want to enjoy all of it, Violet. I've thought about the way you taste since you left my house Monday. But I love that we're here. Now. And we have time to talk. To get to know each other."

Violet met his eyes. She licked her lips, took a deep breath, and finally nodded.

"What?" He tipped his head.

"I didn't want this," she admitted.

"Want what? Steak? Seafood?" He put his menu down. "We can go somewhere else—"

"This." She reached over the table and touched his hand. "Dinner. Conversation. I didn't want to like you."

"No?" He frowned. The waiter chose that moment to appear for their drink order. Bronson ordered a bottle of cabernet sauvignon, but he looked at her for her reaction before handing over the wine list. She flicked her eyes up over the waiter and offered him a smile. Bronson had the fleeting thought that if she hadn't wanted to like him, she definitely had wanted only a fling, and maybe someone like this waiter was more to her liking.

"I haven't dated since the divorce." Her words were a gruff whisper when they were alone again. "I wasn't interested. I was angry with Kody. So mad that he would choose that life over what he promised me. Over life as a dad. In a real family. And then, after the anger went away, I was busy. Being a mom is being busy all the time, but when you have to do the things both parents do, it's even more chaotic and stressful."

Bronson waited for her to go on.

"I'm not complaining. I love Avery more than anything in the world. But it's hard sometimes."

He nodded but said nothing.

"And then...we moved here. And I was busy with settling in and starting the new job and still being Ave's mom. And finally, we were happy and comfortable, and it hit me."

"What hit you?"

She cleared her throat and shrugged.

"You were lonely," he mumbled with a nod.

"I guess."

"So. Is that how you ended up at Frank and Donna's house?"

She licked her lips and winced. "No. Well, I mean, I didn't just tell Frank I was desperate for sex. Just...that as much as I love being here, as good as Avery and I are now…there was something missing."

"And so, you came to a party. Looking for sex."

She winced again. "That sounds so bad."

"Violet, I work those parties. Remember? I know what they're all about."

"Frank told me straight up what it was. Suggested I come and hang out and see what I thought."

"And you thought…"

"I was…overwhelmed. Um…just a mix. Horrified. Curious. Interested. Scared. I've heard of those sorts of parties before. Had friends who talked about them, but…"

"Did you ever have sex at the parties?"

"You know I didn't."

He shrugged and shook his head. Bronson sat back when the waiter returned with two glasses and the bottle of cab. He watched as the kid opened the bottle and poured a bit for him to taste. Bronson felt Violet's eyes on him as he sipped the dry red and nodded his approval. He offered her a sad smile as the waiter poured her wine and then filled Bronson's glass again. They ordered before the waiter walked away, but Bronson's heart wasn't in it now. Not after learning that Violet only wanted sex from him.

"I don't know that. I know you sat at the bar and talked to me. But that doesn't mean you weren't there with someone else at some other point."

"I didn't," she insisted. "I don't think…I could do that. In front of other people."

"I get it," he said quietly.

"But. I saw you. And I thought okay, have a drink and see if that makes you feel differently."

"So, you sat down with me for a drink. To calm your nerves. To see if you could do sex with a stranger and an audience?"

She laughed softly and shook her head. "No. I knew that wasn't my scene. But. I was attracted to you. From the first time I saw you."

Bronson huffed out a sigh. "I like you, Violet. I have since that first night. I had my choice of women to look at, to watch, to fuck. But all I've wanted since the first time I saw you was to spend those evenings flirting with you."

"Why?"

"Because I love your eyes," he mumbled. "Your smile. The sound of your voice. Your laugh."

"Why aren't you taken?"

"What?"

"Why are you single? What's your story?"

Bronson smacked his lips together and took a deep breath through his nose.

"Apparently, single sex is all I'm good for."

Violet flinched at his words.

"I was dating someone. And I thought we were the real thing. I loved her. I was working at the bank with Donna at the time. Jill and I used to go the parties as guests. I guess she enjoyed that more than I realized. When I asked her to marry me, she said no. She wasn't interested in marriage. She liked her freedom. End of story."

"Jill?" Violet whispered.

"Yes."

"The woman you kissed at the last party?"

"The very same."

"She's gorgeous."

"She's pretty," Bronson agreed. "She's got nothing on you."

"When was this?"

"It's been a few years. I quit the bank. I stopped going to the parties. Incidentally, Jill moved. She's back now, but I don't know if she's visiting or if she's home for good."

"She wants you back."

Bronson shrugged. "I'm not interested."

"How long were you together?"

"Couple years."

"You loved her."

"I did." He nodded. "Does something to a guy, Violet, when he reads a woman, a relationship, so wrong. I'll always care about Jill, but I have no desire to be involved with her again."

Violet fidgeted with the stem of her glass.

"You say all the right things."

"Nah." He picked up his own glass. "I say what I feel."

"Did you want babies? With her?"

"I wanted it all with her." He swallowed a drink. "And now, I'm single. And I'm...what am I, Violet? Your rebound? Your bicycle that you're learning to ride again? Your fuck-buddy?"

She swallowed hard.

"I'm scared, Bronson."

"Of me?"

"What I feel for you."

"You said you don't like me."

"I said I didn't *want* to like you." Her eyes filled. She took a second to compose herself. "I liked you enough."

"To fuck me."

Teeth tugging at her lower lip, she nodded. "I invited you over because I wanted to sleep with you. You blew my mind."

"Fuck." Bronson groaned.

"I thought it would be good enough. I thought once would be enough."

"If I scratched your itch, you could keep going for a while."

"I'm sorry."

"Maybe we should've just talked about this up front."

"When you left, all I could think about was the way you made me feel."

"So you've said."

She shook her head. "No. I mean, yes, Bronson, I love the way you fuck me, and I'm wet right now thinking about it. But it's more than that."

"What do you mean?"

"When I'm alone in my bed, and I touch myself and pretend it's you?"

Bronson squirmed in his seat and clamped his teeth together to hold the groan inside.

"When I come? And I roll over and pull a pillow to my chest and wish it was you holding me, I think about the things you say to me. At the parties. Talking about movies and cars and the things you said before we were together. That you like rummy, and your dream car."

"I'm not gonna hurt you, Violet." He shook his head. "And if you're not into this, I'm not gonna force myself on you. I'm not that guy—"

"I know." She cut him off with a laugh that sounded almost like a sob. "I know. You won't. You would never hurt me on purpose. But you might hurt me. And if I let you in, if you meet Avery, and if I like you too much and she likes you, you could hurt her, too. I can't let you hurt my little girl, Bronson."

Bronson rubbed the back of his neck and aimed a frown at her.

"So what? What are we doing?"

"I don't wanna let you go. I don't wanna just let you walk away. Throw you back out there for Jill to grab back. I wanna go home and climb into bed with you. Now."

"But you're afraid of what might happen?"

"Oh, man, I suck." She laughed as she took a big gulp of wine. "I'm sorry, Bronson. I'm being ridiculous. Selfish."

"What if I told you I can wait?"

"With no sex?"

"I can wait," he said again.

"But I want to be with you."

"You're proposing friends with benefits?"

"Is that what I'm suggesting?"

"It's not gonna work," he argued. Violet sobbed softly and propped her chin in her hand.

"Have you seen her? Since that party? Have you slept with her since she's been back?"

"Violet, this has nothing to do with her," he promised. "It's not gonna work because you can't just be friends with me. You can't just fuck me and walk away until the next time."

"I can't?"

"Nope. You're gonna fall in love with me." He grinned.

"I am?"

"Yes, you are." He winked. "I'm gonna bust my ass making sure you fall in love with me."

"Don't bust your ass," she whispered and brushed at her eyes. "Because I'm halfway there already."

10

To Bronson's relief, they spoke often after their first official date. They texted every day. To his delight, they sexted, too. Violet was stingy with details about Avery, but he understood her reticence to involve him in her daughter's life. He hoped someday he and Violet would be close enough that she would trust him to meet Avery, but he was content to wait, as long as he and Violet maintained whatever it was she wanted to call their relationship.

Jill called him often, too. Bronson spoke with her a few times, always happy to say hi and give her the number of a real estate agent—which sounded like she was planning to be back permanently—or give her the name of someone to look at her car when it wouldn't start. But when she tried to turn the conversation to reminiscing or worse yet, flirting, he politely shut her down. When he started letting her calls go to voicemail, she started texting him. Usually quick, silly texts about the woman in front of her in line at the grocery store or memes about dogs or cats. Late at night, she would sometimes text and say she was in bed and thinking about him. Bronson didn't respond to those, but his silence didn't deter her. He would have to talk to her again to let her know he wasn't interested in a second chance.

With the holiday season approaching, he wanted to make plans with Violet. But again, he knew better than to push her. He usually celebrated with extended family; he would be fine doing the same this year. And no matter where he was on Thanksgiving Day and Christmas, he knew he would at least get to talk to Violet.

They spent as many nights together as they could get away with, but never with Avery in the house. The sex got hotter; his need for her grew each time they had to part company. As far as he could tell, Violet felt the same about him, though they never spoke about feelings or commitments.

Having to censor his words, the things he said to her, didn't stop him from feeling for her, though. Bronson was in love with her. He knew he had probably been in over his head with her before he ever took her to bed the first time. Those parties at Frank and Donna's house—the ones where Violet had spent her evenings at the bar with him –had been the most enjoyable he'd had there. Including the times he had been there as a guest, partaking in the sexy fun and games.

The Jacksons had another party before the big holiday bash they were planning for Black Friday. Bronson worked the party, thankful Violet had gone with him. She'd spent the first part of the night on her regular bar stool, but by the end of the evening, she had joined him behind the bar and helped him serve party guests. Bronson loved seeing her come out of her shell and talk to people, but he decided at the end of the night that he preferred having her all to himself. If she was perched on a bar stool, her eyes and her focus were on him all night. Serving drinks put her in direct contact with a lot of tipsy people who had no qualms about having a lot of skin on display.

Violet had giggled and teased him that night when they left the party. When she asked him if he was jealous, he had flat out admitted that he was. He didn't add that he worried now and then about her announcement that she hadn't wanted to become involved with him, that she had only wanted sex. There were still times that he worried she might be biding her time with him, while waiting for something better to come along. Where better to shop for something better than a Wild Canyon Estates Party?

The adventurous sexcapades in his truck later that night after the party did a lot to ease his mind. But he still wished Violet would admit she was in love with him. Or at the very least, tell her mother and friends that they were seeing each other. They were still tiptoeing around her mom, as well as her daughter. That was a bit harder for him to swallow. He didn't necessarily need to meet her mother, but he wanted to know their relationship was serious enough that she told her mom they were intimately involved.

Not in any graphically detailed way.

Black Friday at Wild Canyon would be almost as crazy as retail Black Friday. There would be games. The Jacksons were generous, and there were some fun prizes for the game winners. The top prize for all guests who filled their party passports was a four-day weekend trip for two to Cabo. Bronson wasn't a guest, and he hadn't held a passport in his hands since he'd been coming to the parties with Jillian. But he would have liked to win the trip and whisk Violet away for a weekend of romance.

He had decided to tell Frank and Donna he was ready to hang up his apron and hand the liquor bottles over to someone else. As much fun as it was to hang out there and talk to Violet, everything he and Violet did was fun, and being alone with her topped any party they could have. He hadn't told Violet he had made his decision, though he sensed that she wasn't crazy about him being in the thick of things at the parties. Maybe she felt she didn't have the right to ask him to quit, since she wasn't willing to give him more access to her life and her family. Whatever the case, it was time to move on.

He found Donna in her bedroom, though it felt strange to wander the halls of the house now. The door was open, and with a glance, he could see her standing fully clothed at the dresser. He knocked once, wanting to talk to her before too many party guests arrived. She whirled around, head tilted and hands at her ear as she put an earring in.

"Hey." She offered him a smile. "What brings you to my bedroom?" She wagged her eyebrows at him suggestively and then laughed loud and long. "Because I know you're not looking for sex."

"Yeah? How do you know that?" He tipped his head, curious what people might be saying about him and Violet.

"Well." She folded her arms over her chest and stared at him for a few moments, as if taking stock. "There's the cute little brunette that's been glued to the end bar stool at every party since...September?"

He grinned and dipped his chin, unwilling to say anything regarding his relationship with Violet.

"And there's the sexy woman who's driving back to Rockfield for every party we've had lately, just to get her hands on you. Who's considering moving back, in fact."

"Jill hasn't had her hands on me," he argued. "Not in years."

Donna nodded. "I know. But she sure wants to."

"We talked," he told Donna. "It's not gonna happen."

"What's up?" she asked, turning her wrist so she could see the face of her watch.

"I'm giving you my notice."

"Oh." She drew back in surprise. "Really? Why?"

Bronson filled his cheeks with air and let it out slowly.

"Oh." Donna nodded. "Oh. Because...of the cute...little brunette?"

"You have someone you can give the job to? You and Frank are great to work for and with. But I'm ready to move on, D."

"She doesn't like sharing you?"

Bronson arched his eyebrows but said nothing.

"Oh, come on. You guys are a thing, aren't you? I've seen you making eyes at each other. I know she came with you to the last party."

"Violet and I are good friends," he answered vaguely. "But she's never said a word about me being here. She's never asked me to quit."

Donna sighed and nodded. "Okay. I'll talk to Frank. We'll make it work. Not a problem."

"Good. It's been fun. But." He shrugged.

"Bronson?" she called as he turned to leave her room and head back out to the open living area.

"Hmm?"

"Jill's not gonna take no for an answer," she said quietly. "Not if you and Violet are just good friends."

"It's the only answer Jill's gonna get," Bronson told her. "Come on out. I'll make you a martini."

"Does this mean you're completely off the market now? For me, too?"

"'Fraid so." He winked at her over his shoulder. "Pretty sure you can live without me, D."

Her laughter followed him out the door. Bronson found Violet at the bar talking to Frank. He eyed the man's hand on her shoulder. Wondered for a few moments if anything had happened between them, despite Violet's insistence that she hadn't been with anyone since her divorce. Frank was smiling at Violet but not in a flirty way. Bronson approached

Violet from behind, rested his hands on her hips, and leaned in to kiss her cheek.

"Hello, beautiful."

Violet hunched her shoulders and turned to him with a grin.

"Hello, yourself." She kissed the corner of his mouth.

"Frank. Need a drink?"

"How about a beer?" Frank suggested with a shrug.

"Coming right up." Bronson moved around to the back of the bar and fished a bottle from the cooler. He twisted the top off and handed it over the bar to Frank. "Vi? Wine?"

"Please." She nodded as she propped her chin in her hand and watched him pour a glass of Chardonnay.

"Time to get this party started?" Donna called across the room as she appeared in the hallway. As if on cue, the doorbell rang.

"Here we go." Bronson met Violet's eyes, wondering when he should tell her he was going to quit working the parties. Despite the smile on her face, she seemed distracted tonight, as if she had something else on her mind. Avery had spent the past weekend with Violet's ex, but he thought that had gone well. Could something else be bothering her? He watched her sip her wine and offer him a small smile. Still a bit distracted, but the smile was real enough.

The room filled quickly as party guests continued to arrive. Bronson was a little bit pleased to see Violet involved in conversations with other guests, but it was hard to feel too good about it, knowing that within the hour nearly everyone here would be naked and pawing at each other. Except for Violet, thankfully. Still, he hated that they were here when there were so many other things they could do together. Again, he wondered what she would think when he told her he wasn't going to work the parties anymore. Once he left the house tonight, he had no intention of coming back to a party at Wild Canyon Estates, unless the tone of the parties changed drastically. No judgment, but the parties weren't for him anymore.

With or without Violet Clayton, Bronson was ready to move on.

He was in the middle of making a chocolate martini when he heard Jillian's laugh from the other end of the bar. Bronson shot a glance that way, a feeling of unease gripping his gut when he saw that she was talking to Violet. Dressed in jeans and a button-down blouse—open low to reveal a lot of cleavage—she still managed to look a lot tamer than she had the last few times he'd seen her at a party. She wore just a touch of makeup, and she'd pulled her hair back in a loose ponytail at the nape of her neck. Funny. It was as if she wasn't trying so hard. Bronson thought she looked younger, the same as she'd looked back when they'd been dating. Before the frenzy of skin and sex at these parties had taken over their relationship.

Violet appeared comfortable talking to Jillian, but he couldn't be sure what she was thinking. What if Jill was filling Violet's head with stories about how in love they were and how it was only a matter of time before Bronson came back to her? He and Violet had grown closer, and he was doing his best to change her mind about getting too involved with him. But he wasn't kidding himself; Violet was still being cautious, and too much reminiscing or storytelling from Jillian might send her running.

Bronson served more guests. He managed to talk to each of them as usual, although his heart was at the other end of the bar, worrying about Violet. He glanced her way several times, but she was smiling and talking to Jillian, as if they were involved in a real conversation. A few times he noticed other old friends hovering near Jillian and Violet. Whenever Violet happened to catch him looking at her, she simply offered him that small smile. No wide eyes or look of alarm asking for rescue.

When he finally was able to move down to their end of the bar to talk, he was startled to realize Jillian had pulled up a stool and was now sitting comfortably by Violet, as if she had no intention of moving away and finding her own fun for the night. Bronson topped off Violet's wine, mixed another drink for Jillian, and then propped his elbows on the bar by the women to join the conversation.

"Violet's been telling me about Avery," Jillian told him. "I love that she's learning to play the violin at such a young age."

Bronson did, too, but he hated that he had learned that from Jill, rather than Violet herself. Violet flicked her eyes to his and licked her lips.

"My ex-husband is a musician," she said now, and Bronson wondered if she said it for his benefit. "He played guitar in a jazz band when he was younger. I'm sure that's where Avery gets her musical talent."

"I used to be able to read music." Jillian tipped her head with a frown. "But I hated practicing the piano when I was in high school. I just quit. I don't know if I could still play. Maybe from memory. Not sure I could read music now."

"Kody took Avery to a music show last weekend," Violet announced. "Just a local thing. She loved it."

"That's great," Bronson said quietly.

"So. Bronson, what're you doing for Christmas?" Jillian beamed at him. "I thought we could get together for old time's sake."

Bronson stared at Jillian, dumbfounded by her bold invitation. She knew he was seeing Violet; and if she suspected things between them were in the early stages, she had to know that asking him to spend the holiday with her would offend Violet, if not outright hurt her.

He didn't have specific plans, but he figured he would be with extended family. As much as he cared about Jill, still considered her a friend, he had no desire to spend a holiday with her. Nothing like sending the wrong message to her and Violet.

"Actually," Violet cleared her throat and glanced at Bronson. She appeared perfectly calm, but he thought he knew her well enough to see the uncertainty in her eyes. "Bronson is going to spend the holiday with me. My mom's hosting a small dinner. She'll have some family and a few good friends there, and then me and Avery. And Bronson."

"Oh." Jillian couldn't hide her surprise. Bronson had to work hard to tamp his down, so he understood how she felt. "I had no idea you two were that serious."

Violet pressed her lips together nervously and glanced at Bronson again. She reached over the bar to touch his hand.

"We are," Bronson told her. "I tried to tell you that the other day."

"That's great," Jillian said sincerely. "I hope you enjoy your dinner."

"Thank you." Violet sipped her wine.

"Make sure Bronson makes a pecan pie," Jillian told Violet. Bronson watched her suspiciously as she slipped off the barstool. Was she being sincere, or was she trying to remind Violet that she had a past with Bronson? One that he wouldn't forget? Jillian squeezed Violet's shoulder and then leaned over the bar to kiss his cheek. "Maybe I'll see you for New Year's Eve."

He doubted it, but rather than drag out the awkward moment longer, he kissed her cheek and watched her walk away.

"I would have told her no." He looked back at Violet. "You didn't have to lie."

"It wasn't a lie, Bronson," she said simply. "I'd love it if you joined my family for the holidays."

Bronson arched his eyebrows in surprise.

"You're sure you're ready for that? Me being around Avery?"

"I'm ready if you are."

He grinned and nodded. "I'd like that very much."

EPILOGUE

The yellow disc caught the wind and sailed over Avery's head. Bronson glanced at Violet, who raised her eyebrows and laughed softly. She mumbled something he didn't catch, but Bronson assumed from her shrug that it was something like oops—the same thing she'd said the last three times she'd launched the frisbee over her daughter's head. Avery squealed a small laugh and turned to run after it, but as happened the last three times, the small ball of fur stretched out in the grass distracted her.

"Milo!" Avery dropped to her knees by the puppy and scooped him up to drop kisses over his little brown snout.

Bronson propped his hands on his hips and watched the lovefest between his girlfriend's daughter and the puppy. Milo, a fawn-colored Welsh corgi, climbed over Avery's legs and swiped his tongue up over her nose.

Avery yelped and then giggled.

"He's giving you kisses, Ave," Violet called as she moseyed toward Bronson.

Bronson reached for her and hooked his fingers behind her neck. He leaned in to rest his forehead on hers.

"Can I give you kisses?" he asked with a grin.

"I'd love a kiss, but don't you dare lick my nose." She laughed as she slid her arms around his waist.

"You let Milo lick your nose," Bronson reminded her.

"Milo has those big puppy dog eyes, though." She shrugged and tipped her face up to kiss the corner of his mouth.

"I thought you liked my eyes."

"I do, Bronson Hart, but you have bedroom eyes. Not puppy dog eyes."

"Bedroom eyes, huh?" He couldn't help the grin.

"Mom, can we take Milo for a walk?" Avery called. Bronson and Violet both looked her way, though neither of them moved to put space between them. They'd been dating now since November. Though they'd been open with Avery since Christmas at Violet's mother's house, they were careful about the affection they displayed for each other around her. They shared a lot of tender touches and kisses, but they didn't sleep together when Avery was at home.

As much as Bronson wanted the freedom to take Violet any time and any way he wanted, he didn't mind. In fact, he enjoyed being around Avery; the kid was smart and sweet, and her laugh lit him up inside. They'd become something of a unit, though neither he nor Violet had discussed the future in any definite words. They'd never even whispered the L word, though Bronson was head over heels in love with her and ninety-nine percent sure she felt the same for him.

"I suppose," Violet answered. "Why don't you run inside and use the bathroom first?"

"But I don't have to—"

"Avery." Violet cocked her head as the girl climbed to her feet. "Please do as I asked."

"Will Bronson read me a story later?" Avery arched her eyebrows.

"You need a bribe to take Milo for a walk?" Violet snorted.

"No, to go to the bathroom." Avery rolled her eyes now and then turned a sweet face to Bronson.

"I would love to read you a story," he promised her. "But only if you help me."

Avery grinned and dashed by him to go inside. "Be right back, Milo!" she called as she ran.

"You don't have to do that," Violet reminded him when they were alone.

"I like reading to her." Bronson shrugged and tugged Violet back in to stand close to him. "And I like to hear her read."

"She loves it when you listen to her read," Violet whispered.

"We're almost through the lastest Magic Treehouse book."

Violet pressed her cheek to his chest and smoothed her hands over his back.

"Do you miss it, Bronson?"

"Miss what?"

"The parties."

"No."

"No, I mean…" Violet pulled back to look at him. He winced when he saw that old uncertainty in her eyes again. "I know you like being here, and you have fun with Ave. But you're a guy. Do you miss the sex and the things you saw at the parties?"

"Vi—"

"I don't want you to be bored taking me to bed when you could have any of those—"

"Violet Clayton, have I ever appeared bored taking you to bed?"

She bit her lip, but she couldn't hide her sly grin.

"No."

"How about when I take you on the kitchen table?"

"No."

"In the shower?" He tipped his head.

Violet snorted and shook her head no.

"I don't miss it," he promised her. "I don't wanna be anywhere else but here with you and Avery."

Violet met his gaze and stared at him intently for a long moment.

"Why do you ask?"

"Hmm?"

"I'm thinking we've got a pretty good thing going here." Bronson brushed her hair back from her face and stroked his fingertip over her cheekbone. "What makes you ask about the parties? You lookin' for something new?"

This time her smile was soft and sweet. "What could I look for that's better than what I have?"

Bronson groaned and splayed his left hand over her lower back to pull her snug against him.

"I saw Donna the other day at the mall," Violet told him. "We talked a bit. She asked how you're doing."

"And you said?"

"I said you feel good." Violet grabbed his ass and gave him a squeeze.

"Do I?" He laughed.

"Everything about you feels good," Violet promised. "She said Jillian had moved back to town."

Bronson nodded. "She told me that."

"Jillian did?"

"Mm-hmm."

"Do you still talk to her a lot?" Violet sounded a little alarmed by the thought.

"No. She finally quit calling me after you announced to her last year that I was spending Christmas with your family. And she quit texting after she asked if I baked a pecan pie for the dinner and I said yes, but you and I ate it in bed and had a whipped cream fight."

Violet threw her head back and laughed. "Did you seriously say that?"

"No, because it's none of her business what you and I are doing, Violet. And because I don't want to be hateful. What I'd like is to know that Jillian finds someone to love her the way I love you."

Violet pressed her lips together and arched her eyebrows.

"So when did you talk to her? When did she tell you she'd moved back?"

"She came into Riptide one evening. Maybe it was her last stand? I don't know. But I told her I'm happy. That you're my future. I think she got it."

Violet licked her lips and nodded, but she kept her gaze trained on his chest now. Bronson's heart thumped wildly in his chest. Those big words had ramped his heartrate up to speed demon, and her lack of response made it plummet so fast, he was almost dizzy.

"Donna told me they're having a big Fourth of July party next month. She invited us."

"I don't wanna go, Violet." He shook his head.

"Do you like fireworks?"

"Yep. I'd rather watch some with you and Ave, and then make some of our own later."

Violet nodded, chin still tucked her to chest. She slipped her arms around to his front, though, to rest her hands on his chest.

"Bronson?"

"What?"

"You told me once that you wanted everything with her." Violet cleared her throat. "With Jill."

"Violet—"

"Marriage. Babies. The whole family thing."

"Sweetheart, I don't love her," Bronson said firmly. "Do you really doubt—"

"Do you still want everything?' she whispered. She lifted her eyes to meet his. "With me?"

Bronson blew out an anxious sigh. "I want more than everything with you."

"Babies?'"

"You know I'm crazy about Avery, right?" He cupped Violet's chin in his hand. She gave him a small nod in response. "And I would love to be a permanent part of her life, too? I love you both, Violet."

Violet licked her lips and tipped her head. "I love that you love her," she said quietly. "You're so good with her. But…do you want your own child?"

"I would love to be a dad. To Avery."

"Bronson." She groaned.

"What?"

"I love you." Violet rubbed her fingers over the scruff on his chin. "I want to make you a father. With Avery, yes, but I wanna be with you. I wanna have babies with you. I want to wake up with you every day, and I wanna listen to you read to Ave every night, and I wanna hear our children call you Daddy."

Bronson swallowed hard.

"You deserve that, because you're so good with my baby girl."

"Damn, Violet." He laughed, though his eyes burned. He blinked and nodded. "Are you proposing?"

Her soft laughter warmed his heart.

"Did I propose, or did I proposition you?"

"Seeing as how we're already having incredible sex, I think the proposition ship has sailed."

"Then I guess that leaves a proposal."

Bronson threaded his fingers in the back of Violet's hair and pulled her close for a kiss.

"I'm ready, Mom!" Avery banged the door open and rushed back into the yard to grab Milo's leash.

"Do you have an answer?" Violet pecked Bronson's cheek with a quick kiss.

"Did you tell Donna we would be at the Fourth of July party?"

"Well, I told her no. Thanked her for the invite but told her we had other plans."

"Good." He nodded. "And we do."

"What are we gonna do?"

"Violet, I'd rather throw a frisbee with you and Avery and take Milo for a walk and read about a magic treehouse and time traveling kids than go to that party."

Avery walked back by them, leash in hand. Milo followed behind her, stopping to sniff every other blade of grass.

"Really?" She beamed at him.

"Or we could get married." He shrugged and turned her so they could follow Avery around the garage and down the driveway. "And then after we watch the fireworks with Avery, we could light some of our own and see about making one of those babies."

Violet leaned into him as they walked.

"How do I love you so much?" she wondered out loud.

"Well, I did warn you," he reminded her.

"You did, didn't you?" She looked up at him and laughed. As they followed Avery and Milo down the street, Violet walked on her tiptoes to kiss Bronson's cheek.

"One thing." Bronson squeezed her waist and kissed the top of her head.

"What?"

"No wedding shower at Frank and Donna's house."

Violet's laugh drew Avery's attention, but the little girl

only rolled her eyes at Violet and turned her attention back to Milo.

"I don't need a shower. I don't need gifts. Don't need anything but you and Avery. And Milo."

"And a honeymoon." Bronson wagged his brows at her and shot her a lecherous grin.

"Oh, God, yes, I'm gonna need an annual honeymoon with you, Bronson Hart."

SNEAK PEEK AT LIPSTICK & LIARS

Chapter 1

Ava

When you take your wedding ring off after wearing it for nineteen years, you're making a statement. It's interesting to see the way people react. Some do a double take, like they have to be sure they saw a bare ring finger when you were talking about the new program you're working on, and you were gesturing wildly because taking your ring off wasn't natural for you and you forgot you did it, and so you don't think anything about it or try to hide it. Some try to be sly about it. They double take. They sneak a peek at your hands again when you stop talking and you're reaching for your wine glass, and some turn to look at a colleague, and they try to be sly about this, too, but you see the curve of their eyebrow, and you know they're thinking *did you know? What's that about? Have you seen Logan? Is he wearing his ring?*

He's not. Logan took his ring off first, and I didn't even notice until we were packing for this trip to Dallas. We're in the same industry, so we travel together often. Used to be fun, but honestly, it got old after ten or twelve years. Take a fun, whirlwind romance and throw in bills and money and kids and all the drama kids can add to life, and let's not forget exhaustion, and those trips stop being a luxurious get away and become one more thing on the calendar. Kind of like making love. Should be fun, adventurous, special. Instead, it gets stale, and you resent the time you give to your partner because you just want a little *me* time.

Then again, it's not like that for guys, is it? Sex is *me time* for men, especially when they can roll over and go to sleep when it's over.

Logan was folding his button-down shirts to pack in his suitcase. He's a stylish guy—always has been—and I stopped what I was doing to watch him. The shirt he was holding was new, gray and white checked. I looked from the shirt to what appeared to be a new gray sport coat tossed over the end of the bed. Logan continued to pack, oblivious to my interest. I had my hair dryer in hand; I had planned to ask him to stick it in his bag as mine was jammed full.

"Mia's counselor—" I stopped midsentence. I remember that. Watching him as he packed his stuff meticulously. Thinking that he had a better wardrobe than I did. He keeps his fingernails cut blunt and clean. His hands are big and strong. And for nineteen years, he's worn a white gold wedding band on his ring finger.

"What about Mia's counselor?" he asked without looking up at me.

My heart hurt.

Not figuratively. Not like flowery-poetic-love-story-heart hurt. It hurt like when your ob-gyn presses and squeezes your ovaries during a pelvic exam. Pain that's sharp and severe and then when he releases you, you feel a little crampy and uncomfortable.

When I still couldn't speak, Logan piled the gray and white shirt on a pale blue shirt—folded just as perfectly—in his suitcase and looked up at me. He wears glasses sometimes instead of contacts, and recently, he switched from the wire-rimmed rectangle lenses he's worn for years to fashion frames.

My husband of nineteen years was dressing like a twenty-year-old guy and not wearing his wedding ring.

Yes, before you ask, I'll just tell you. We're going through some things. At twenty-five, when we got married, I was naïve enough to believe we were different. We were wildly in love and crazy about each other, so there wouldn't be any bad times. Nineteen years later, I know better. Show me a marriage without strife, without growing pains and blow ups, and I'll call bullshit.

ABOUT THE AUTHOR

TE Sheridan loves to read—anything—loves to write—again, she would rather not be nailed down to one particular genre —and loves to travel. She and her happily-ever-after love live in the Midwest, have two children, and live & love life to the fullest.

Writing under her other name—the one that recently decided to experiment with some new, grittier ideas and a pen name—TE is the author of thirty women's fiction and contemporary romance novels and recently decided to experiment with a pen name. As TE Sheridan, she is the author of the Wild Canyon Estates Stories. Lipstick & Liars is her first stand-alone contemporary romance novella.

ALSO BY TE SHERIDAN

www.ingramcontent.com/pod-product-compliance
Lightning Source LLC
Chambersburg PA
CBHW030546130626
46552CB00006B/2445